THE LIVING DEAD

She was where she had been a moment ago. But nothing was the same. The sun was coming up, not going down. The air was still, the cemetery neat and tidy. She climbed slowly to her knees. What had happened? She remembered a branch falling, but when she glanced up, she could see no place where a limb had broken off. She couldn't find the flowers she had brought for Mike.

"Where am I?" she whispered.

She touched the soil beside her. That, too, had changed. The earth was looser than it had been when she arrived, as if it had just been dug up and shoveled back over a coffin.

"Mike," she whispered.

It looked so very fresh.

She stood and began to back up. "No, Mike."

Fresh as a body that had just been buried.

The brown soil on top of the plot began to stir.

"Stop it, Mike!" Jean cried.

Something poked up through the brown earth into the air.

Books by Christopher Pike

BURY ME DEEP
DIE SOFTLY
FALL INTO DARKNESS
FINAL FRIENDS: #1: THE PARTY
FINAL FRIENDS: #2: THE DANCE
FINAL FRIENDS: #3: THE GRADUATION
GIMME A KISS
LAST ACT
REMEMBER ME
SCAVENGER HUNT
SEE YOU LATER
SPELLBOUND
WHISPER OF DEATH
WITCH

Available from ARCHWAY Paperbacks

Christopher Pike

Bury Me Deep

AN ARCHWAY PAPERBACK
Published by POCKET BOOKS

New York   London   Toronto   Sydney   Tokyo   Singapore

AN ARCHWAY PAPERBACK *Original*

An Archway Paperback published by
POCKET BOOKS, a division of Simon & Schuster Inc.
1230 Avenue of the Americas, New York, NY 10020

ISBN: 0-671-69057-4

First Archway Paperback printing August 1991

10 9 8 7 6 5

AN ARCHWAY PAPERBACK and colophon are registered trademarks of Simon & Schuster Inc.

Cover art by Brian Kotzky

Printed in the U.S.A.

IL 8+

FOR MIKE, MY NEPHEW

Bury Me Deep

CHAPTER

ONE

"Trans Island flight one-oh-one to Maui," the speakers in the airport lounge called out. "Please board now."

That's me, Jean Fiscal thought. *That's my plane.*

She was going to Hawaii for spring vacation, and it was totally awesome. As she stood up to board the jet, Jean gulped down the remainder of her Coke and danish. Paradise was waiting. She grabbed her carry-on bag and purse—checking for the tenth time that she had her ticket—and hurried to the gate. She had never been to Hawaii before. She had been born and raised in Los Angeles and had never even been out of California.

"How long till we take off?" Jean asked the burly flight attendant as he checked her boarding pass. He glanced at her, amused by her excitement.

"Sometimes they roll you out onto the runway and leave you there for hours," he said.

Jean laughed. "You're a lousy advertisement for your company."

"You don't know how right you are. I've never even been on a plane."

"Are you kidding?"

He shook his head. "I've worked here fifteen years and seen too many of them crash on takeoff."

Jean gave him a knowing nod. "I guess the smell of the burned bodies gets to you after a while."

He finally laughed. "Yeah, that's it exactly." He handed her back half the boarding pass. "You have a nice safe trip. Have fun while you're at it."

"Thanks. I'm already having fun."

Passengers were backed up in a small knot at the door leading to the plane. This was no business flight. Dress was casual. Half the people had on Hawaiian shirts. They were all chatting about the things they were going to do on the islands. Jean remembered the guidebook she had bought the previous week. She'd have to finish reading it on the plane. It was presently six in the morning. The flight was five hours long, but because of the time change, she'd land in Maui as early as nine. She wasn't even going to lose half a day traveling.

But that's hardly a bargain. I've already lost two days of my vacation.

It was Monday. Her two friends, Mandy Bart and Michele Kala, had left for Hawaii on Saturday, two days earlier. She was supposed to have flown with them, but her chemistry teacher stopped her. Friday, in the middle of a major acid-base reaction exam, her mom had called the school to have her go home. Apparently their dog—her name was Spotty, and she was a snow white retriever without a

2

spot on her—was in the middle of delivering a half-dozen puppies. Jean hadn't known what to think. She was fond of Spotty but thought her mom was overreacting and treating Spotty like the obedient daughter she had never had. Anyway, she told her mom to call the paramedics. Her mom was not amused and ordered her to get home that instant to help her or else she would never forgive her.

So Jean drove home. When she got there, twenty minutes later, Spotty was the proud mother of *seven* puppies and doing just fine, thank you. Her mom was so relieved she gave Jean a huge hug. Back at school, thirty minutes after that, Jean was told by her chemistry teacher to come in on Sunday afternoon—and only Sunday afternoon—to make up her exam. He had plans that couldn't be changed. The alternative was to take a big F on the test. The teacher wasn't totally unconcerned about trips to Hawaii and six-month-old plans, but his life was more important than Jean's. Since Jean was a conscientious student and planned on going to college to major in something that would make her a ton of money, she agreed to the conditions without any violent threats. Barely.

Her teacher really wasn't a complete jerk about the situation, though. He had a doctor friend write her a note explaining to the airline that her sinuses had been too clogged to fly the previous Saturday. With the note Jean had been able to change her flight to Monday morning without paying extra. This was important to Jean because she was traveling on a tight budget. She had earned the money for the trip all by herself, working as a survey girl at the local mall. The pay fit the job—both were lousy.

"Hi! My name's Jean Fiscal! May I ask you a few questions? Thank you so much! Do you eat Jell-O? Do you like strawberry or lime? How much money does your household take in in a year? Does your husband like Jell-O? What flavor? Grape? Oh, no, it's different from your favorite! How long have you two been married?"

It was amazing how many people she spoke to actually considered each question carefully before responding.

At last the crowd at the door thinned out enough, and Jean went inside. The cabin was warm, hot even. She began to perspire, and she only had on baggy green shorts and a white cotton blouse. Her seat was 37A. She asked a smartly dressed middle-aged flight attendant named Patricia where it was.

"In the back on the right," Patricia said.

"Is that by the window?" Jean asked.

"Yes," the flight attendant replied, stowing what looked like a golf bag in an overhead compartment with a door that was threatening to fall down and bite off her right arm. "Have you flown before?"

"No." Jean frowned. "Does it show?"

"No," Patricia said. "It was just an educated guess. Please take a seat as soon as possible. You're blocking the aisle."

It shows. I've got to stop smiling. I've got to be cool.

Jean found her seat and stowed her carry-on bag under the seat in front of her. She wanted easy

4

access to it because she had brought—besides her tourist guide—a number of other books to read. She was currently into big trashy Hollywood novels. She told herself that she read the books because everyone else did, and she wanted to be able to discuss them in social situations. Actually, she just liked the dirty parts. She had an idea that she would no longer enjoy reading about sex after she had done it. So she wanted to gather as much written information beforehand. Mandy and Michele said there were boys in Hawaii, lots of boys.

I'm not going to do it, though, no matter what he looks like. I'm not a tramp. Then I'd have to read my chemistry textbook on the flight home.

Jean might not have wanted to lose her virginity in Hawaii, but she wanted to come close. She longed for romance. Oh, she'd had boyfriends—two of them to be exact. Ted Deeds had been the first. They'd met two years ago, when she was sixteen and he was twenty. He'd been an older, experienced man. He was so experienced that on their first date he confided in her that he wanted to enter the seminary and become a priest. She should have known he was a losing cause right away. A priest, for Godsakes! She had to wait two months and eight dates before they made out, and then she just *knew* the whole time they were kissing that he was thinking about what his penance would be when he went to confession the next day. It ruined the whole experience for her.

Then there was Bob Falst, dear confused Bob. On the surface he appeared to be a normal warm-blooded American boy. He was eighteen and horny, and he looked pretty good, too. She met him in her doctor's office. She was there with a bad case of something the doctor never diagnosed, but which shortly went away. Bob was there because—she was to learn this much later—he was a hypochondriac.

Bob liked to make out. They made out in his car a dozen times. But about half those times she *hurt* him. She didn't mean to. She wasn't sure how she did it, or when, or even exactly what she did to him. But by God he would suddenly be in tremendous pain, and he would let her know it was her fault. Bob was a paranoid hypochondriac. They could be in his car kissing passionately and he would lean slightly forward and herniate two disks in his neck. Just like that. He had the physiology of a scarecrow, and her embrace was like a blue torch across his straw guts. She never went all the way with Bob. She figured he would need a brain transplant if he had real sex.

So that was her love life—pathetic. Her demands were very reasonable at this point. She just wanted to meet a guy who hadn't heard the voice of God and who didn't spend his nights counting the germs in his bedroom. She figured Hawaii would be the place.

At last the plane was ready to take off. As they taxied away from the terminal, Jean was pleased that the seat beside her was still unoccupied. She had been up late the night before packing and was hoping to take a nap during the flight, which would be easier without close company. The empty seat appeared to be one of the few on the plane. In fact, as far as she could tell, it was the only one.

The runway wasn't crowded. They only had to wait a couple of minutes before they were in position to take off. As Jean buckled up, she gazed excitedly out the window. The jet engines began to whine and then roar as they pushed the giant plane forward. The feeling of speed was exhilarating. Jean felt herself being pushed back in her seat as they tore down the runway. Then, all at once, they were in the air, and it was like magic that something so big could fly with the birds. The hotels and other buildings surrounding the airport shrunk beneath them. Within seconds they were out over the ocean.

Then both the ground and the ocean vanished. L.A. was covered with overcast that morning. They were in the air less than fifteen seconds when they entered a gray cloud. Up and up they climbed, and the featureless gray remained. Jean began to feel cheated. It was her first flight, after all. She decided it was good she hadn't had to pay extra for a window seat.

But she was still happy. She watched attentively—she appeared to be the only one doing it—as the flight attendants demonstrated what to do in case of emergency. She paid attention to all of the captain's announcements, particularly the one that said they would probably arrive twenty minutes early. Another twenty minutes of vacation! She knew she was going to be sick at heart when she boarded the plane late next Sunday to return home, and even sicker when she woke up for school the following morning.

The flight attendants came by—Patricia was taking Jean's aisle—and offered everyone a beverage. Jean requested bottled water. She was a cola freak but knew the caffeine would keep her awake. Now that the excitement of takeoff had worn off, and she knew the clouds were going to stay for a while, her fatigue hit her. Lunch and the movie weren't scheduled until the second half of the flight. If she was going to sleep, she decided, now would be the time. Fetching a pillow and blanket from the overhead compartment, she curled up in a ball in the seat, her forehead resting on the window. She was out in a minute.

CHAPTER
TWO

She awoke with the *feeling* that someone was sitting beside her. The person in question hadn't touched her in any way or spoken to her, but she knew— even before she opened her eyes—that someone was there. She felt something else, too, in that moment—a chill. It was slight. It passed over her body like a wisp of autumn fog and was gone almost before she recognized it as having been there.

She turned her head slightly and was looking at Mike.

He appeared to be about her age, eighteen, and his hair color was similar to hers, light brown. But there the resemblance ended. Jean was tan—she went to the beach often—and had classic California good looks. Her smile was absurdly bright. Her dad had never given her a penny of allowance while she was growing up, but he had sent her to an expensive orthodontist. Her hair was very shiny, and she wore it long, straight down her back. Both

Ted and Bob had commented on the softness of her brown eyes. Apparently, she looked sweet even when she was about to explode in anger, which she did only when someone tried to take advantage of her. She was nobody's fool, except perhaps when it came to boys, who, of course, she could never get to take advantage of her.

The fellow sitting beside her didn't have typical good looks, but she didn't hold that against him. She preferred interesting-looking guys, and he certainly was different. There was a gentleness in the lines of his face, an innocence. He had a frail build and carried himself carefully. He looked as if he had seen little of the outside world. His pale skin shone even in the poor light coming through the cloud-clad windows.

"Hi," Jean said.

He jumped slightly when she spoke, as if he were unaware that she was there. His eyes were light brown, creased at the edges with faint sad lines. He glanced quickly over at her.

"Hello," he said.

Jean smiled. "Where did you come from?"

Her question appeared to confuse him. "I was sitting here."

"Have you been sitting there awhile?"

He hesitated. "Yes."

"Have I been asleep a long time?" she asked. Her watch seemed to have stopped.

"Yes."

Jean yawned. "I don't mind you sitting here." She gestured to the small movie screen off to their right. "We'll have a good view of the movie. Do you know what it's going to be?"

"No."

"I hope it's one I haven't seen. I go to practically every movie. I work at a mall. They have ten theaters there. I sneak into them all the time. Do you go to the movies much?"

"Never," he said.

"Really? Where are you from? Is that a southern accent I hear?"

He relaxed and smiled, and even though his eyes remained sad, his smile was warm. "I'm from Hoker, Alabama. It's a small town, back in the hills. There isn't a movie theater there."

"Wow. What do you do for entertainment?"

"I go for long walks in the hills. I bring my rifle with me."

"Do you go hunting?"

"Yes."

"Do you shoot animals and eat them?"

He nodded. "Raccoons mainly. They taste good cooked over an open fire." He added, "I never shoot anything I don't eat."

"Oh, I think that's fine—hunting for food, I mean. It's just that I never met anyone who did it before." She chuckled. "Around my neighborhood we have grocery stores."

"We have a grocery store in Hoker. But it's a poor area. The store is small, and we can't always buy everything we need."

"You sound like real survivors to me. I admire that." She offered her hand. "My name's Jean Fiscal. What's yours?"

He shook her hand, his grip feeble. "Mike. Mike Clyde."

"Pleased to meet you, Mike. Are you traveling alone?"

"Yes."

"So am I. Isn't this great? Going to Hawaii, I mean? I've been looking forward to it for months. How about you?"

He frowned. "What?"

"Are you excited about going to Hawaii?"

He thought a moment. "Yes. I've been looking forward to it for a very long time."

"I'm glad we're going to Maui instead of Oahu. I've heard it's real crowded in Honolulu. Are you going to any other island besides Maui?"

"No. Just there." He smiled faintly. "Maui is the best."

"That's what the old adage says. Where are you staying?"

Mike reached inside his shirt pocket and withdrew a heavily creased piece of colored paper. If she felt she was dressed casually, he was ready for a hunting expedition into the hills of Alabama. His blue jeans were worn to pale gray, almost white, and his gray shirt was frayed at the cuffs. The short olive green boots on his feet could have been purchased at any Goodwill. He silently studied the piece of paper in his hand, which he seemed to hold with unusual delight.

"The Island Suites," he said. "It's on Kaanapali Beach."

"That's where I'm staying! That's amazing. What are you going to do when you get there?"

Like the inquiry of a few moments earlier, the question was normal enough, but it caught Mike off guard. She had to repeat it for a second time, and then Mike's gaze suddenly shifted far away.

"I'm going to go in the ocean," he said softly.

"Well, of course you are. Maui is surrounded by ocean. But what else are you going to do?"

He refocused on her. "I've never been in the ocean before."

She felt like a fool. "I'm sorry, I shouldn't have said that the way I did. I'm a California girl. I grew up beside the ocean. I assume everyone goes in it all the time. Have you ever seen it before?"

"No. But I've seen it in pictures." He gestured to the colored paper in his hand. "They sent me pamphlets when I won the trip."

"You won this trip to Maui? God, you are one lucky fellow. I had to work my tail off for months to get to go."

Mike nodded, showing his excitement. "They were having a contest in a magazine I found at our local drugstore. I tore out the coupon and sent it in. I didn't even have to buy the magazine. And then, two months later, they sent me a letter and said I could go to Hawaii. They sent me an airplane ticket and everything." He nodded once more. "We get to stay at the nicest hotel in all of Hawaii."

Actually, their hotel was supposed to be very good, but she knew for a fact there were far more expensive hotels on Maui. Yet she saw no reason to contradict him since he was obviously so happy about the prospect.

"It's going to be great," she said. "But can I ask

you a stupid question? You don't have to answer if you don't want to. Do you have pools in Hoker?"

"No."

"Then can you swim?" she asked.

"There's a lake not far out of town that I swim in all summer. I'm a good swimmer." He turned away from her, again gazing off into the distance. Once more the sadness in his expression struck Jean. When he spoke next, he was merely repeating what he had said a moment earlier, yet his tone was different, somehow lost. "I'm a good swimmer."

Jean felt unclear where he was coming from. "I'm sure you are."

He briefly closed his eyes. When he spoke next, it was as if he were speaking to himself. "The lake I learned to swim in is nice, but it doesn't have the water Hawaii does. In Hawaii the water is clean and deep. You can go as deep as you want. You can go down and down, and never get to the bottom."

Jean smiled nervously. His last remark had sounded so gloomy. "You do get to the bottom eventually."

He finally turned to her again. But his attention didn't cause her to relax. It was as if he were seeing right through her.

"When the moon is full, it lights up the water at night," he said. "You can see the dark fish. You can see the caves of colored coral. The fish swim in the caves, and the tide rushes out. When the time is right, the water rushes through the moonlight to the end of the cave."

The chill Jean had felt upon awakening suddenly

returned, only now it was far colder and deeper—it was the coldness of the moonlit waters he was describing. He was spooking her, and she wanted to know why. She wasn't easily unnerved. Maybe it was because he was talking firsthand about a place that he had never visited, and he was staring at her with a strange light in his eyes. Yet that didn't completely explain her feelings to her satisfaction. There was something else that was happening. . . .

Or something that was about to happen.

An odd thought. What could happen aboard a modern plane? She hastily glanced out the window, and then back at Mike. The feeling of impending doom remained. It was as if one of the dark clouds through which they were passing had seeped into the cabin and was now hanging above them, waiting.

Waiting?

Mike's pale skin took on an ashen tone.

He just sat there, staring at her.

"Is there something wrong, Mike?" she asked carefully.

"You're sitting in my seat," he said flatly.

"No. This is my seat. But if you'd like to sit here, you're welcome to." She paused. "Are you sure you're all right?"

He took a deep breath. "Don't I look all right?"

"No. I mean, yes, you look fine. But you're talking a little strange. What is this moonlit cave with the rushing tide? Did you read about it in one of the pamphlets they sent you?"

He took another breath and coughed weakly. "No one talks about it. It's just there. It's a place.

The water rushes in and it's warm. It passes through the rays of the moon. When it rushes out, it's cold." He coughed again, harder this time. He spoke with effort. "I shouldn't go there."

Jean leaned over and patted him on the back. "Are you OK? Should I get you a glass of water?"

He closed his eyes, this time grimacing in pain. He seemed suddenly to become confused. He buried his head in his hands. "Why is this happening again?" he asked desperately.

Jean sat up straight. "What's happening? Talk to me, Mike! Are you feeling ill?"

He rolled his head toward her, and his hands dropped to his chest, which he hugged tightly, as if he were trying to hold himself together. Sweat glistened on his forehead and dripped salt into his suddenly bloodshot eyes.

Is he having a heart attack?

Mike's eyes bulged, and his skin took on a faint blue tinge.

"Help me," he moaned as he sucked in a thin, ragged breath.

"Try to relax," Jean said, panic sweeping through her. Her own heart was pounding, and as she tried to hold him with both her hands, the conviction that there was something wrong with his heart grew. He was obviously having difficulty breathing, but more than that, he was now shuddering with horrible muscular spasms. He hugged his ribs tightly. It was as if his heart were going to explode any second, out through his rib cage, and spray them both with blood.

"Somebody help us!" she cried.

16

In seconds they were surrounded by people: Patricia the flight attendant; a tall man in a business suit; another flight attendant. Together they tried to hold Mike as huge convulsions rent his body. He was no longer merely shaking and gasping for air. Now it seemed as if he were being torn apart by some unseen force. His whole spine arched, and he was thrown into the aisle and onto the floor.

"Help him!" Jean screamed.

"He's having a seizure!" Patricia yelled. "Hold him still."

The two men grabbed Mike's upper torso and tried to pin him down. For a moment they had no luck, he was thrashing around so violently.

But then Mike suddenly stopped and became still.

A faint sigh escaped his lips, as the final breath left his body. He lay calmly on his back. A drop of blood appeared at the corner of his mouth. Jean stared at it as it rolled over his chin and onto his neck, tracing a fine red line. It was only one drop; there were no more, but it was enough. Mike stared toward the ceiling of the airplane with vacant and fixed eyes.

"No," Jean whispered.

Patricia leaned over Mike and began CPR. The flight attendant appeared adept at it. She breathed for Mike, she pumped his heart. She did these two things for what seemed an eternity, but Mike just kept staring at the ceiling without seeing it.

Finally Patricia sat up and met the worried faces gathered around her. "He's gone," she said.

"Yes," Jean whispered. She sat back in her seat.

She stared out the window at the gray nothingness. There was no sky, no ocean. There was no world for Mike or herself. She turned her head back to his body. People were once more sitting down. Mike continued to lie where he had fallen. A flight attendant appeared with a green body bag.

I was just talking to him, God.

The flight attendant lay the body bag beside Mike. Patricia helped her partner roll the body inside. A strand of Mike's brown hair momentarily caught on the bag's zipper as they pulled it up over his face. They managed to tug it free.

Just a few minutes ago we were talking.

Then Mike was gone. They carried him away. Patricia paused beside Jean as she walked back toward first class. She put her hand on Jean's shoulder, and they met each other's gaze for several moments without speaking. Then Patricia's eyes began to water, and she hurried away.

I knew him just a few minutes.

Jean turned away and rested her forehead on the window, curling herself into a ball beneath her blanket, assuming the same position she had when she had begun her nap. She closed her eyes. Yet it was odd that she continued to see gray clouds. They swam in her mind like vaporous chemicals trying to delude her brain. She saw something else, too—a pale moon inside the clouds, floating in a sky pulsating with white bubbles. Cold white bubbles that sparkled as the moon shone through them.

CHAPTER

THREE

Jean didn't wake up until the plane was preparing to land. An announcement from the captain made her sit upright. He was telling the passengers to fasten their seat belts. She opened her eyes and was immediately blinded by the intense glare of the sun. The clouds were gone. Shielding her eyes, she caught a glimpse of wide, warm blue below. They had reached Maui. Her dream vacation was about to begin.

But Mike. What about poor Mike?

His horrible death seemed a dream to her now. She couldn't get over how he had appeared in her life, made himself a part of it with his sweet and endearing expression, and then vanished. But it was no dream. When the plane had come to a complete stop, and the people were filing out the twin exits, Jean passed the flight attendant named Patricia. Once more their eyes locked.

Jean sniffed. "It was sad about Mike."

Patricia paused. "Did you know him well?"

Jean shook her head. "Barely. I had just met him." She paused. "It was just horrible that he had to die so young."

Once more Patricia's eyes moistened. She touched Jean's shoulder. "He was a nice kid. He was so excited about his trip to Hawaii."

Jean nodded. There were people at her back. She had to get out of their way. She had to get off the plane. God, how she hated the plane. It was like a huge silver coffin now.

"Thanks for what you did for him," Jean said.

"I didn't do anything for him," Patricia said, and there was a note of self-recrimination in her voice. "What's your name?"

"Jean Fiscal."

"I'm Patricia."

Jean nodded at her name badge. "I know."

They exchanged goodbyes and best wishes. Jean trudged toward the exit, her carry-on bag a lead weight over her shoulder. She felt physically and emotionally drained. No one she knew had ever died before. Death was not a subject she had given much thought. People died on TV and in movies. They weren't supposed to die in the real world.

My world isn't real. I'm a flake. All I cared about when I got on that plane was having a good time.

But was that so wrong? Mike himself had been looking forward to having a good time. Perhaps it had been a blessing that he had gone so swiftly, with no idea that his end was so near.

But maybe that wasn't true.

"Why is this happening again?"

He had said that just before he died. He must

20

have had a serious medical condition. Jean marveled at his bravery at embarking on such an extensive vacation when he was obviously not well. Mike must have been a person who believed in trying to get the most out of life. She wondered if there was a chance he would be buried in Hawaii, and if she could go to his funeral. She sort of doubted it; his family would no doubt want his body returned to Hoker, Alabama. She decided to call the airline the next day to see what arrangements were being made.

Jean stepped off the plane and walked down the steps. The jet had parked a distance from the terminal, and she had to walk across a hundred yards of airfield to reach the baggage area. The air was warm and humid, but not uncomfortably so. A sweet fragrance filled her nostrils. It was undeniably the smell of paradise. She was going to have to try her best to put what had happened out of her mind and enjoy herself.

Of course, she knew it would be impossible to forget Mike Clyde.

Jean was surprised to see that the baggage area was outside. She could never have imagined such a thing. Didn't it rain almost every day in Hawaii? That's what the guidebook had said. Apparently, Hawaiians were not bothered by the moods of the great outdoors.

Jean collected her suitcase and scanned the area for Mandy, without success. Jean wasn't unduly concerned. The plane had arrived early, and Mandy was traditionally a few minutes late. She was probably Jean's best friend, certainly her oldest one. They had known each other since elementary school. Mandy was a chatterbox but knew how to listen well, too, and they got along with at most two bad arguments a year. Mandy was a fascinating combination of brilliant and dumb. Her wit was the quickest in the school, but when it came to grades, she could only joke about how unnatural it was to be educated.

"Aloha!" Jean heard in her ear a few minutes later as she felt a flowered lei being dropped over her neck. Mandy had sneaked up on her from behind. Jean turned to find Mandy with a tan that looked more like two weeks than two days.

"What does *aloha* mean, anyway?" Jean asked after giving Mandy a quick hug.

"Hello, goodbye, let's have sex," Mandy said. "I don't know. Everyone says it here."

"Is everyone here having sex?"

"Michele maybe," Mandy said. "Probably. She's a fast mover. How was your flight?"

Jean hesitated. "It was all right. Where's the car? I want to sit down."

Mandy gestured to the parking lot. "Over there. But you've been sitting for hours. I would have thought you'd want to stretch. Hey, you look kind of tired. Do you want me to carry your suitcase?"

"Yes. Thanks." Jean handed the bag over with a twinge of guilt. Mandy was big-boned, but she was not particularly athletic or strong. A tall girl, with short brown hair and straight bangs, she had a plain and dizzy expression until she laughed. Then she looked positively insane. Mandy had a lot of friends. She had a lot of friends who were boys. Yet, like Jean, she didn't have *a* boyfriend. She was so vivacious, she just mowed them over, and no one could take her seriously. At least, that was what Jean thought, but what the hell did she know.

They walked to the car, and Jean was surprised to find they had rented a red convertible. Back in L.A. the three of them had decided on an economy car. For Jean money had to be a constant consideration. But Mandy was quick to defend her and Michele's choice of cars.

"It only cost a few dollars more for the whole week, and the man who rented it to us said you have to have a convertible if you want to see Maui. He was right. It's great driving along the ocean. You'll see."

"Then you were able to use the car rental coupon they gave us at the travel agency and apply it toward the car?" Jean asked.

They had purchased the vacation as a package deal. They had coupons for all sorts of things: meals, boat rides, helicopter trips. The trouble was, they didn't have enough coupons for all the possible activities. For example, if they went for a boat ride to Lanai—a small island off Maui—they couldn't go snorkeling at Molokini, a submerged volcano also off Maui. They had to plan carefully, which Mandy liked to do about as much as she liked homework. Jean worried that Mandy and Michele had already wasted some of their most valuable coupons.

"Absolutely," Mandy said, tossing Jean's suitcase in the backseat of the convertible and unlocking the driver's door. "Don't worry about it. It was a hundred bucks more for the whole week. That's nothing."

That was thirty-three dollars more that they each had to fork over, assuming Mandy was not underestimating the charge. Climbing in beside Mandy, Jean wondered how she could be counting dollars and cents when she had just watched a young man die. Then she realized that was exactly why she was doing it. She was grasping at anything real and concrete so she wouldn't have to think about the solitary drop of blood that had rolled out of Mike's mouth when he had let go of his final breath. She shivered at the memory of it and found her own breath hard to draw in. Then she felt a light touch on her arm. Mandy's voice was concerned.

"What's wrong, Jean?" she asked.

Jean burst out crying. The tears just flooded out, and for several minutes she just sat and let Mandy hold her. Mandy was wise that way; she knew when it was best to be quiet. Finally, though, Jean was able to tell her about Mike Clyde—the sad-eyed boy with the two first names. She started at the beginning, when she woke up to find Mike beside her, and ended with the green body bag. Mandy's face grew dark at that point. She shook her head, incredulous.

"What could it have been?" Mandy asked when Jean finished.

"Probably a heart attack, maybe a stroke," Jean said. "I don't know. He could have had epilepsy the way he thrashed about. All I can say is I've never seen anything like it, or even read about it. The

attack just grabbed him and"—Jean sniffed—
"didn't let go of him until he was dead."

"The poor guy. You said he was about our age?"
Mandy asked.

"Maybe a year or two older. I'm lousy with ages."

"You only got to talk to him for a few minutes?"

"Yeah." Jean gestured helplessly. "But there was
something about him. He was neat. I was happy
when he told me we would be staying at the same
hotel. I thought all of us could get together with
him." She cried more. "How can things like this
happen?"

Mandy was sympathetic. "But it's as you said.
He was happy he was going to Hawaii. It was the
high point of his life. Don't you think, if you had to
go, that you'd want to go when things looked bright
and beautiful?"

"I understand what you're saying," Jean said. "I
guess I just have to push it out of my mind."

"Don't do that," Mandy said seriously. "If he
was as nice as you say, it's good to remember him.
Talk to me about him any time you want."

"Thanks," Jean said, and she meant it. Talking
about the incident had made her feel better.

They drove toward Kaanapali Beach and their
hotel, which was on the west side of the island,
forty minutes away. Like the other Hawaiian islands, Maui had a diverse climate. On the wind-
ward side it rained constantly. That was where the
tropical forests were located. They would no doubt
visit there, but they were staying on the leeward,
where the fabulous beaches were and where most of

the tourists went. There it also rained, but not nearly so much. As they drove away from the airport, Jean marveled at the pineapple plantations that stretched out from the road. She felt silly having thought that pineapples grew on tall trees. These were low, stocky plants.

The fresh air was divine. It seemed richer in oxygen, more nourishing than L.A. air. Jean was glad for the convertible. When they reached the coast and turned right toward the hotel, she was able to see the small islands of Molokai and Lanai at the same time without ducking out a window. The water was a stunning clear blue, and looking at it soothed the emotional turmoil inside Jean. She was about to turn back to Mandy when a huge dark shape broke the surface about a quarter mile off shore.

"Mandy!" she shouted in delight. "Look at that!"

Mandy grinned, keeping her eye on the road. "Is it a whale?"

"I think so. It just jumped up like Moby Dick himself. It's gone now. Have you seen any whales?"

"Dozens. Apparently, the humpbacks come down from the Alaskan water to have their babies in the bowl created by Maui, Lanai, and Molokai. Here the water is calmer and warmer. We're lucky. They're supposed to leave in a couple of weeks. You'll see a lot of them when you go out on a boat."

"Have you and Michele already been for a boat ride?" Jean asked, immediately returning to her concern over their limited number of coupons.

"Yeah, we were out whale watching yesterday."

Mandy glanced over. "I hope you don't mind that we went without you."

"No," Jean lied.

"We didn't use any of our coupons," Mandy hastily added, lying. "We met these two guys who had a boat. They took us out."

Jean knew that *we met* really meant that Michele had met. Michele was a blond beauty. The boats were probably lined up in the harbor to take her to exotic secluded beaches. Michele was not a close friend of either Jean's or Mandy's. They had only gotten to know her when she had decided to accompany them to Hawaii. Michele had sort of invited herself on the trip.

"Tell me about them," Jean said.

"Their names are Dave and Johnny. They work at the hotel as scuba instructors. They take people who aren't certified scuba divers and give them enough skills in the hotel swimming pool so they can go on an ocean dive. They teach a class every other day starting at eleven o'clock." Mandy paused. "The three of us are signed up for today's class."

Jean looked at her. "What?"

"You'll like it. They're neat guys, and you'll learn how to breathe underwater. You're not mad, are you? Tell me you're not mad."

"Do we have to use a coupon to take this class, or are they going to teach us out of desire for our bodies?"

"The boat belongs to them," Mandy said. "But when they teach, they do it through the hotel. We'll have to use a coupon."

"But then we can't go on a helicopter ride," Jean complained. She had wanted to take a helicopter over the big volcanic crater—Haleakala. Her guidebook said it was one of the island's best bets.

"We can still go on a helicopter ride if we don't go parasailing," Mandy said.

"But I wanted to go parasailing." Parasailing was like waterskiing, except a parachute was tied to the skier's back so the person would go flying way up in the air.

"We can't do everything," Mandy said. "We discussed that already."

"We discussed that we would decide what to do—as a group—when we got here. Anyway, I don't know if I can scuba dive. I suffer from claustrophobia."

"Since when?"

"Since someone told me I have to go underwater in a couple of hours," Jean said.

"It's only the pool class that's in a couple of hours—we won't do the ocean dive till later this afternoon. Trust me, Jean. You'll like the guys. Dave's a fox and Johnny's a real sweetheart."

"How old are they?"

"Dave's twenty-one," Mandy said. "Johnny's a year older than us, nineteen. They've lived on the island all their lives."

"I assume Michele's already got Dave wrapped around her finger?"

"Or wrapped around other parts of her anatomy." Mandy was another virgin, rich in fantasy but lacking in experience. "They're probably doing it as we talk."

Jean smiled. "Underwater?"

"Probably in our room."

"Who gets Johnny?"

Mandy beamed. "He's mine."

"You sound pretty sure of yourself, sister."

Mandy lost her smile. "I'm serious, Jean. I like him. Would it be OK, you know, if you laid off him?"

"I don't recall ever hitting on anyone you were interested in."

"I mean it."

Jean was surprised at her tone. "Sure. I won't even look at him. Tell me about the hotel?"

"It's great. There's a wide-screen TV in every suite, and a video rental store downstairs. Our balcony looks right out over the beach. The couch folds out into a bed. The bed in the bedroom's huge. We can both sleep in it, or have a cot brought in. Whatever you'd like."

"I'm flexible. But I don't know if I want to take this scuba class."

"Jean."

"I'll think about it," Jean said.

They arrived at the hotel twenty minutes later. Island Suites was located about a mile from Kaanapali's other hotels. It was painted a toylike orange and had a gorgeous waterfall running down the front facade. Every room had a balcony, and those suites that didn't face the ocean had views of lush green hills. Jean felt a pang as they drove up to the reception area. Mike would have loved it.

Jean checked in while Mandy parked the car. She was given a key to her room and a pass that would allow her to charge food and drinks. She didn't have to bother about her bag; a bellhop appeared and whisked it away before she could protest. She would have preferred to take the bag up herself. Bellhops expected to be tipped.

Jean wasn't given a chance to go straight to the room because Mandy reappeared and wanted her to see the pool first. Jean should have suspected it wasn't the pool she was being dragged off to meet.

It was Johnny.

He was sitting high on the lifeguard seat when they walked up. Jean's initial impression of him was that he was a beach bum. His hair was dirty blond, and if it had seen a comb once that spring it had been lucky. He was beautifully tanned, and his long thin legs were well muscled. Indeed, his whole body appeared a solid sinew of strength, even though he was slender. His expression—at present bored by the monotony of staring at a practically empty pool—seemed to be full of fun. He would be a guy for a wild weekend of fast cars and warm beers. He smiled and looked over when Mandy called out his name.

"Hey, Mandy," he said. "You were able to follow my directions to the airport, after all. Is this your friend?"

"Yeah," Mandy said. "This is Jean. Jean, meet Johnny."

Johnny leaned down from his perch and offered his hand. Jean had to look into the glare of the sun to reach it. This guy had a strong handshake.

"It's nice to meet you, John," Jean said.

"Johnny, please. It's nice to meet you." He let go

of her hand. "I heard you're going to be diving with us at eleven."

"Maybe," Jean said.

"She just got here, you know," Mandy said, shifting her attention between the two of them. "She should probably take it easy at first."

My, isn't that a change of tune.

"Are you worried it might be dangerous?" Johnny asked Jean.

"Not exactly," Jean said. "I just worry about breathing while I'm underwater and choking."

Johnny nodded. "I can't tell you that won't happen. Scuba diving is a serious sport. But if certain precautions are taken, it can be a safe sport. Remember, my partner and I will be within arm's reach the whole time you're underwater."

"We'd actually go diving in the ocean this afternoon?" Jean asked.

"Yes," Johnny replied.

"I told you," Mandy said, obviously wishing to be a part of the conversation.

"I'm surprised," Jean said. "I'd have thought it would take a lot more training than we could get in a single class."

"Thousands of people take these short courses every season on Maui," Johnny said. "We haven't had one fatality yet."

"I think she's scared," Mandy said.

Jean leveled her gaze at her friend coolly. "You know I don't scare easily."

"Think about it," Johnny suggested. He checked his diver's watch. "We're not going to start for an hour. If you don't want to do it, don't let anyone talk you into it. You have to want to do it. But I can tell you this. It's more fun than anything you've ever done in your life."

Jean laughed easily. Already she liked Johnny. "I'm glad you're not trying to talk me into it."

He laughed, too. "Maybe I am, a little."

"Hey," Mandy broke in. "Why don't we go up to the room?"

Johnny gave a wry grin. "Michele and Dave might be up there."

"I hope we don't surprise them," Jean said. "Nice meeting you, Johnny."

"Nice meeting you, Jean."

Mandy was on her as soon as they got in the elevator. "I thought we had a deal," she said, hurt.

"What? I asked him a couple of questions. So what?"

"So what if he likes you?"

"He doesn't know me. How can he like me? You're being paranoid."

The elevator had glass walls. Mandy stared down at the open central courtyard as they rose toward the tenth floor. "We'll see," she said.

At the last second, just before they entered the room, Mandy realized she had left something down by the pool. Jean wondered if she was eager to get back to Johnny and repair what damage supposedly had occurred. Mandy quickly excused herself. Jean hoped the events of the week didn't turn into those of a TV soap. She took out her key and unlocked the door. She did not knock.

The suite was as beautiful as the brochure had promised. There was a small kitchen, a large entertainment console, and a wide balcony. The door to the master bedroom was closed. Jean moved to the balcony and stepped outside. She stretched in the bright sunlight and drank up the view. Directly below her was the one-acre pool, surrounded by lush tropical plants. The beach in front of the hotel was packed with sunbathers. The waves were not as high as she expected, but they were smooth as glass. People of all ages, boogie boards under their bellies, rode in and out on the surf. In the distance she could see the small islands of Lanai and Molokai, smooth mounds of green rising from the dazzling blue of the sea.

"This is heaven," Jean said, sighing. She leaned over the balcony to see if she could spot Mandy talking to Johnny.

It was then a wet hand touched her back.

"Ah!" Jean screamed. Her shock was so great that she almost fell over the balcony. The wet hand grabbed her shirt firmly and pulled her back. Jean whirled around to find Michele standing there, wearing nothing more than an orange hotel towel.

"Did I scare you?" Michele asked.

"You did." Jean put a hand to her pounding chest. "I almost fell over the balcony."

Michele stepped to the edge of the balcony beside Jean. She had it all: the blue eyes, the full chest, the brown skin, the long blond hair. It was only the shape of her mouth that was questionable. Besides being small, it had a slight tendency to twist down on the right side when she smiled. Then again, Jean had heard guys at school say that Michele Kala had the most devilishly sexy smile.

"You shouldn't have been leaning over so far," Michele said, gazing down at the people on the beach.

"I suppose you're right."

Michele glanced over at her. "How was your flight?"

Jean hesitated. "Fine. How's paradise?"

Michele laughed easily and raised her arms, risking the possibility of her towel falling down. "Exotic. I love this place. You know I stayed in this hotel the last time I was here?"

"That's what you said. Mandy tells me you've already found a boyfriend?"

"I didn't find him. He found me." She tilted her head back. "Dave! Come meet Jean, my friend from L.A."

A powerfully built young man stepped onto the balcony from the bedroom. His hair was black, cut short, and he wore a tight black bathing suit. He could have been a body builder. His brown muscles glistened with sweat in the bright sunlight. His eyes were an intense gray; he stared at Jean for several seconds before his face registered any emotion. When he spoke, his voice came out deep and firm. He seemed older than twenty-one.

"My name's Dave," he said. "Michele's told me about you."

Jean smiled. "Was it all good?"

"I told him you were an interesting person," Michele broke in. "Interesting people are seldom all good." Michele glanced at Dave and batted a couple of lovely eyelashes. "That's why I'm fascinating. I'm completely wicked."

34

"What have you guys been up to?" Jean asked.

Have you been having sex? Did I interrupt? Was it good?

"We were getting to know each other," Michele said, amused.

"Michele," Dave said, not pleased.

Michele shrugged her shoulders, and her towel slipped a notch. Another inch and Dave would see her bare breasts, not that he hadn't probably seen them already.

"Jean's cool," Michele told Dave.

"I understand you teach the scuba diving classes here at the hotel," Jean said to Dave. "I just met your partner, Johnny. He was telling me about it. I'm thinking of taking it."

"I thought she was taking it," Dave said to Michele, ignoring Jean for a moment. Michele, in turn, chose to ignore Dave.

"Let's just do it," Michele said to Jean. "It's a groove being underwater."

"You've scuba dived before?" Jean asked, surprised.

Michele hesitated. "No. But I can imagine, you know." Then she laughed again, in her carefree manner. "If you don't take the class, I'll be very disappointed. Say you'll do it."

Jean stared out at the ocean again. It was so clear, she could see the coral bottom. But it would be nice to see it up close.

"I'll do it," she said.

CHAPTER

FOUR

An hour later Jean was sitting beside the pool with her friends. Since making her decision to take the course, Jean had managed to down a quick lunch. The hotel food was excellent but expensive. A turkey sandwich, fries, a piece of cake, and an exotic fruit smoothie called a tropical delight had cost what dinner for two in a family restaurant would. She had charged it to her room, but wondered if that was such a good idea. The bill at the end of the week might floor her. Perhaps she should just pay for everything as she went along, she thought. At least then she'd know exactly where she stood.

She envied Michele, who had eaten an early lunch with her and Mandy. Michele ate all she wanted and never gained a pound. And she had her daddy's credit card to charge anything she desired.

Apparently, the three of them were the only ones taking the course. Dave and Johnny labored nearby with five scuba sets. The equipment looked heavy.

Jean said as much to Johnny as he stepped by her on the pool deck.

"They're heavy on land," he said. "But in the water they're weightless. Everything is."

"Wow," Mandy said. "How is that possible?"

"The buoyancy of the water is responsible," Johnny said. "You'll love the sensation once you're under."

That was the only information they received from Johnny for a while. Dave was the one who actually taught the class. While Dave spoke, Johnny checked out all the equipment. But occasionally he would glance up, and Jean believed he was glancing at her.

He is kind of cute.

Mandy had said nothing at lunch about the love rivalry.

Jean's initial impression of Dave's stern manner had been accurate. He was a no-nonsense instructor, and Jean didn't mind one little bit. She wanted someone who took the matter seriously. She was still more than a little nervous about breathing underwater.

"We're going to learn four basic skills before we dive in the ocean this afternoon," Dave began, standing waist deep in the water in front of them. He held up a snorkel and mask. "First, you have to learn to clear your mask underwater. No matter how well a mask fits, some water is bound to leak in. This is a skill you must master. Fortunately, it's not complicated." He put the mask down and reached for the mouthpiece. "Second, you will learn how to clear your regulator. No matter how careful you are, sometimes your regulator is knocked out of your mouth." He let go of the regulator. "Then you must learn to clear your ears. You probably all did this once or twice on the way here as your plane began to descend. But in diving you have to clear your ears many more times. In fact, if you can't clear your ears properly, you will not be able to dive. Finally, we will learn to swim using fins. Are there any questions so far?"

Jean raised her hand. "How long will we be underwater when we do go in the ocean, and how deep will we go?"

Dave picked up a large silver air tank. "Each of these tanks carries three thousand psi—that's pounds per square inch. We will each dive with one tank. How long it lasts depends on how much you weigh and how easily you breathe underwater. An experienced diver can usually dive longer with the same amount of air, because he or she is more relaxed. On the whole, women can stay underwater with a tank longer than men. But to give you a rough idea, we'll probably be under about forty minutes. On an introductory course like this, we don't go any deeper than forty feet. Personally, I prefer to take people no deeper than thirty feet."

"Thanks," Jean said.

"How many know what *scuba* means?" Dave asked.

"Self-contained underwater breathing apparatus," Michele said. She had a killer pink French bikini on. Jean wasn't even trying to compete. She had opted for a green one-piece, figuring it would handle the dive well and stay in place.

"You're so smart," Mandy said sarcastically.

Dave nodded. "How smart you are isn't important in scuba diving. What matters most is how cool you are, that you don't panic. This is the rule: Think, then act. If you remain cool, you'll be perfectly safe no matter what happens." Dave reached once more for the face mask and snorkel. "But let's start with the skills."

Dave had them each take a face mask. They had to suck in a breath through their noses while the masks were on their faces to see how well they held, or fit. None of them had a problem. Dave went on to the mask clearing.

"Just press with the palm of your hand on the top of the mask and exhale through your nostrils while tilting your head back," he said, demonstrating the move. "The pressure of the air inside your mask will force the water out the bottom of the mask. It's important that you exhale slowly. If you blow too hard through your nose you will injure your eardrums. Let's try it a few times sitting here at the edge of the pool. We'll practice all these skills before we get in the water."

They tried out the move. Jean could see the logic of it and found it easy. Mandy had a little difficulty, however, and required a few pointers from Dave. But Jean thought Mandy was faking the difficulty to get more attention.

They moved on to the next skill—clearing the regulator. For this Johnny set up a unit of scuba equipment beside each of them. Jean tried to lift hers off the deck and found it difficult. The ease with which Johnny handled the equipment impressed her. He smiled as he lugged the stuff around. It was obvious he loved nothing more than being outdoors, in the sun, in his shorts.

"There are two ways to clear the regulator," Dave said, his own equipment floating in front of him in the pool. He had pushed some kind of button on the equipment, which had inflated a black vest attached to the air tank. Jean assumed that was why it wasn't sinking.

Dave continued. "There is the blow method and the purge method. You will practice both." He held up the big black mouthpiece, which was part of the regulator. "Say your regulator is kicked out of your mouth by your partner, or it falls out, which it never should do unless you're trying to sing underwater. Because you are underwater, you can't just put it back in your mouth. You have to clear the water out of it before you can inhale from it again. If you don't, you'll choke, which is unpleasant when you have thirty feet of water above your head."

Jean shuddered slightly. That was precisely her fear. She glanced at Mandy and Michele. Neither appeared to be concerned. She raised her hand.

"Is this something we have to worry about?" she asked. "I mean, is it likely to occur on just one dive?"

"No," Johnny said from his position twenty feet to the right.

"It probably won't," Dave said. "But people do

40

lose their regulators. Last week I had a man lose his while he was descending. His wife was above him on the rope, and she kicked it out of his mouth."

"What did he do?" Jean asked.

"He did exactly as I had instructed him to do," Dave said. "And he was fine. Let me demonstrate the skills. They'll give you confidence. I'll start with the blow method." In a single smooth move Dave put his arms through the inflated black vest and swung the whole pile of equipment over his head. In a moment he was buckling his belts and seemed to be ready to dive. He raised the regulator in front of his mouth. "I'm breathing comfortably, enjoying the underwater sights. Everything is fine. Then suddenly my regulator is gone." He tossed the regulator over his shoulder. "What do I do?"

"Scream for Dave," Michele said.

Dave didn't smile. "The regulator comes from the right side. It's the same on all the equipment we use here. So what you do is lean to the right with your whole body." He did so. "And sweep with your right arm, all the way back. If you don't lean first, there's a chance you'll miss the regulator hose." Dave let his arm slide under the hose, and then followed the hose back to the regulator. Once more he held it up in his hand. "Now I've said this before, but I'll say it again. You can't just put it in your mouth and start breathing. You must get rid of the water in it. You do it by putting it in your mouth and blowing hard." Dave did so, then began to breathe off the regulator. He sounded like Darth Vader with it in his mouth. "See how simple it is? Now I want you to practice with each other. Don't put the equipment on your back yet. Just lean to the side as if it was there, and grab the regulator when you want to blow."

They practiced it several times. Then Dave demonstrated the purge method. It was the same as the other method until the point when the regulator was in the mouth. Then, rather than blow the water out, they used the purge valve on the back of the regulator to get rid of the water. It was easier, and yet it had a catch. A diver had to be sure to block any water from coming in to his mouth. Dave demonstrated how to use the tongue—when the purge valve was pushed. Jean found the different techniques interesting.

Finally they came to the part about clearing their ears. Dave gestured to the sky. "The hundred or so miles of atmosphere we have above us creates a pressure on us of one atmosphere," he said. "But if we go just thirty-three feet underwater, we will have two atmospheres of pressure on us. This is because water is so much heavier than air." Dave gestured to the side of his head. "There is an air space inside our ears. If the pressure inside it is kept the same as the pressure outside, our ears feel fine. But if the pressure outside increases, and the pressure inside remains the same, we feel pain. For that reason, as we go deeper underwater, we must clear our ears every two feet."

"Every two feet?" Mandy asked. "But two feet of water is nothing."

Dave pointed to the water. "This pool goes down eight feet. If you were to dive to the deepest part and stay there for even a minute, you would be surprised at the pain in your ears. We clear every two feet because it is easier to clear our ears when we're experiencing no pain. If, while descending in the ocean, you feel the slightest pressure, clear your ears immediately. If they don't clear, go up a couple of feet, then try again. There are three methods people use. One is to pinch your nose and blow lightly. Notice I say the word *lightly*. If you blow hard, you can injure your eardrums. You can see how your masks have been designed to allow you to pinch your nostrils shut. The second method is to swallow repeatedly. The third is to wiggle your jaw around. Most people use the first method until they have more experience. This is a skill we'll have to practice in the water. Are there any questions?"

"Can you clear your ears too much?" Jean asked.

"No," Dave said. "But you can clear them too hard. You understand?"

"Do you have to clear your ears while you're coming back up?" Jean asked.

"No," Dave said. "Usually your ears equalize naturally. But I'm glad you asked that question. How we return to the surface is important. Let's talk about pressure some more, and how it affects our lungs." He pointed to his chest. "Our lungs are like big air sacks. As we descend in the water, the air in our lungs must be more compressed to hold up to the greater external pressure. The regulator takes care of that problem for us automatically. That's what its there for. So when we are thirty-three feet under the surface, the air in our lungs is twice as compressed, twice as thick. But say we want to come back up to the surface. Say we want to come quickly. What would happen if we did so holding our breath?"

"The air inside our lungs would expand," Michele said.

"That's correct," Dave said.

"How did you know that?" Mandy asked.

"It's obvious," Michele said. "The air would expand and our lungs would rupture."

Jean grimaced. "Is that true?" she asked.

Dave nodded. "If you rushed back to the surface from even thirty-three feet without breathing, you would probably suffer an air embolism. An air embolism is the most common injury in scuba diving."

"Is that what they mean by the bends?" Jean asked.

"No, that's something else," Dave said. "We don't have to worry about the bends—which is nitrogen bubbles forming in the blood—on a dive this short and shallow. Neither will we have to worry about nitrogen narcosis, which can happen to divers at depths greater than a hundred feet. That is also related to nitrogen in the blood."

"Can an air embolism kill you?" Jean asked. The sport was sounding gloomier all the time.

"Most definitely," Dave said. "For that reason the number-one rule in all of scuba diving is that you must *keep breathing at all times*. That might sound silly. Why would you want to stop breathing? But you'd be amazed at how many people have a natural tendency to hold their breath as they move back toward the surface. You must breathe

the whole way up, and you must go up slowly. Any questions?"

"Has anyone you've taken on these dives ever suffered an air embolism?" Jean asked.

Dave hesitated. Johnny spoke up. "No," he said. "Never."

"That's good to hear," Jean muttered.

It was time to practice all the things they had learned in the pool. Jean was surprised how cool the water temperature was. They were in the tropics, after all. Mandy reassured her that the ocean was much warmer.

They didn't don their equipment until they were all standing in four and a half feet of water. Johnny had been right about the buoyancy of the water. Jean found the equipment somewhat confining, but she hardly noticed its weight. They put on their masks. Johnny fussed behind her head with the valves and adjusted the cummerbund that helped hold the tank on.

"Are you comfortable?" he asked.

"I feel fine," she said, still a little nervous.

"I think my stuff is too loose," Mandy said. Johnny moved to help her, and Mandy became instantly happy. Dave called for their attention.

"Now we're going to sink under the water as a group," he said. "We will drop to our knees. Our heads will only be a couple of feet below the surface, but you'll probably all have to clear your ears."

This is it. I'm going to breathe underwater.

Or choke.

They stuck the regulators in their mouths. It tasted like rubber to Jean. She also found it not entirely easy to breathe from, but figured that was part of the game.

Dave checked them out. "Is everyone okay?"

They all gave him a thumbs-up sign. Dave gave them a thumbs-down.

They let themselves sink under the water.

The first thing that Jean noticed as she slipped beneath the surface was how loud the Darth Vader sound had become. Then she became amazed and fascinated with how clearly she could see underwater. Although she lived near the ocean back home, she had never been snorkeling before. She had never even seen underwater with a mask on. It was a real treat. Everyone did look buggy-eyed in their masks, though, and she had to force herself not to laugh.

I'm doing it. It's easy.

As Jean settled to her knees with the others, she was amazed by how simple it was. All she had to do was remember to breathe through her mouth and not her nose. She watched with delight as the bubbles rose from her regulator.

But there was definitely pressure on her ears. Despite Dave's warning, she was surprised. A couple of feet had seemed like nothing. Dave gestured to his ears, and she immediately reached up and pinched her nostrils shut through the flexible plastic that surrounded her nose. She blew lightly and the pressure vanished.

Dave gave them a few minutes of breathing easily and then gestured that they were to allow water into their mask. Jean's nervousness quickly returned. If there was water in her mask, she might accidentally suck in some through her nose. Then she'd gag. The thought made her want to stand right up.

Just relax. Everyone is doing it. You can do it, too.

Johnny shifted over and was directly in front of her. He smiled, and with his regulator in his mouth he looked like a Martian. Like Dave, he gestured for her to tilt open the top of her mask. She did so timidly, letting in a trickle of water. He nodded for her to continue. She cracked the top seal a tiny bit farther. Cold liquid poured over her cheeks and swam over her nose, drowning it. She had to fight the urge not to breathe in through her nostrils even though she knew that would be the worst thing she could do.

What am I supposed to do?

Skills that had been so simple two feet above the surface were suddenly difficult two feet below. Johnny pressed the top of his mask, then she remembered.

Think, then act.

Press, exhale slowly through the nostrils, and tilt the head back. That was it. She tried the technique, and as if by magic, the water disappeared from inside her mask. Johnny offered his hand, and she shook it vigorously. She felt absurdly pleased with herself.

Michele had no trouble clearing her mask, but Mandy had a hard time. They all watched as she tried again and again, but the water stayed in her face. Jean could see she was getting flustered when Dave took her by the hand and brought her back to the surface. When she sank back under two minutes later, she seemed calmer. She cracked her mask and let a little water in. Then she slowly blew it out. Jean recognized what her problem was. Mandy had been blowing too hard, all at once.

Now Dave wanted them to take a breath, blow out bubbles, and throw their regulators over their shoulders. He demonstrated the leaning-to-the-right technique and the two ways of clearing the mouthpiece once it had been found. Jean found this skill much easier than the mask clearing. As on the surface, she preferred the purge method to the blow method. Once more, Michele performed the skills effortlessly, and again, Mandy had difficulty. When she took the regulator out of her mouth and threw it over her shoulder, and couldn't find it, she panicked and jumped right back up to the surface. Dave motioned for them all to come up.

"That is exactly the kind of reaction I don't want to see in the ocean," he said firmly. "Never bolt to the surface. Handle the situation where you are, whatever it is."

"But I didn't have my air," Mandy complained. "I couldn't find the regulator."

"Take a deep breath," Dave ordered her. "Now blow out slowly. Continue to blow. See, you have enough air to blow for a while. But just now you searched for your regulator for only five seconds before you panicked. Remember—think, then act."

Jean took the regulator out of her mouth. "But what if your regulator gets knocked loose while you're inhaling?" she asked.

"Then you may begin to choke," Dave said. "But keep this in mind—you have air with you. You don't need to run to the surface to clear your lungs. You don't want to. Now I'm going to take Mandy back down. We'll practice until she's comfortable. You other two relax on the surface."

Mandy and Dave went back under. Johnny watched them from the surface, a hint of concern on his face.

"Do you think she'll be OK in the ocean?" Jean asked.

"We'll see," Johnny said evasively.

"She just needs more practice," Michele said.

Jean shook her head. "She shouldn't go unless she's comfortable with the basics."

Michele nodded, distracted. "Where are we going to dive this afternoon, Johnny?"

"We'll be diving off the beach not far from here," he replied. "It's a nice spot. The coral's good and there are plenty of fish."

"What's the mile marker?" Michele asked.

Jean had noticed mile markers on the road to the hotel. Mandy had explained that it made spots easy to locate. Someone could just say, "Go to mile marker so and so."

"Number twenty," Johnny answered. "Why?"

"Just wondering," Michele said. She turned to Jean. "How do you like it so far?"

"It's bitchin'," Jean said.

"You're not scared, are you?" Michele asked.

"No," Jean said.

"Wait till you get out in the ocean," Johnny said. "You'll love it."

"What are we going to do next?" Jean asked.

"Swim to the deep end and practice the proper kicking motion," Johnny said, still watching Mandy underwater with Dave.

"Can't *you* show us how to do it while we wait?" Michele asked.

"Dave's the boss," Johnny said.

"Does that ever bother you?" Jean asked.

Johnny just shrugged. "He's older," he said. "He owns more of the boat than I do."

"When we do a shore dive, we don't go on a boat, do we?" Jean asked.

"No," Johnny said.

Dave and Mandy finally surfaced. Mandy continued to look unsure of herself, but Dave seemed satisfied. They moved on to the final pool phase. Dave had them each grab a pair of fins from the side of the pool and put them on. Now they were going to swim with the scuba equipment on.

"When diving," Dave said, "you don't want to use your arms to swim. They'll just slow you down. Use your legs and try not to bend your knees too much. Keep your legs straight and your arms by your sides. Johnny, you take Jean, and I'll take Michele. We'll swim down to the deep end and make a few circles. Mandy, you stay here and rest for a few minutes."

"I'm not tired," Mandy said quickly.

"I want you to rest," Dave said.

When Jean started to put her mask back on, she noticed the faceplate was fogging. Johnny told her to spit in it and rub the spit around the clear portion.

"Isn't that kind of gross?" she asked.

Johnny smiled. "It depends on your perspective. You can use dishwashing detergent as well. But spit will work for now. Rinse it off in the pool when you have finished rubbing it into the faceplate."

She did as she was told and was surprised that it worked perfectly. She put her regulator in her mouth, and Johnny dropped an extra lead weight in a pocket in her vest.

"That's to keep you from bobbing to the surface," he explained. "We'll go into this in more detail before we go into the ocean. How much do you weigh?"

"A hundred and ten pounds," Jean said.

Johnny turned to Mandy, who was still catching her breath. "How about you?" he asked.

"A hundred and fifteen," Mandy said, telling a twenty-pound lie.

Johnny took Jean's hand and again slipped beneath the surface. The lead weight helped. She went straight to the bottom of the four-foot section of the pool, and immediately felt the need to clear her ears, which she did. She noticed something about the regulator. It was easier to breathe through when she was underwater.

They began to swim toward the deep end. There was no one else in the pool except them— understandable since the ocean was supposed to be so much warmer. The lead weight might have been helping too much; it was difficult for her to stay off the bottom. Johnny reached over and pressed a button on a black hose on her left side. She heard a squirt of air and felt the vest that held the tank on her back tighten. She figured the button regulated her buoyancy. Immediately she bobbed off the bottom, going neither up nor down, floating somewhere in between.

This is great!

She swam lazily into the deep end and for the first time in her life experienced the feeling of weightlessness. Johnny let go of her hand and encouraged her to roll onto her back and look up. Silver bubbles streamed from her regulator toward the shiny surface. It was so neat! She felt like a little kid.

Then Dave came along and snapped his fingers at her. He pointed to his locked leg. He wanted her to practice the proper kick, and no fooling around.

Jean began to swim in slow circles around the deep end. Michele swam in front of her, but quickly got so far in front that she was behind her. The guys hovered in the middle, never taking their eyes off them. Jean was having a great time. She was happy the others had talked her into taking the course.

They practiced the kick for maybe ten minutes, then Dave gestured for them to surface. But the moment Jean began, Dave grabbed her arm and violently shook his head. He indicated she was to go up slowly and look where she was going. Once more she didn't mind his strictness. When they were finally on the surface, Dave reached over and pushed the button that put more air in her vest. She found she could float in the deep end without even having to move her fins.

"Come up no faster than one foot a second,"

Dave said to both her and Michele, who was also floating on the surface. "That may sound fast, but it's not. It's very, very slow."

"But other than that we did great, huh?" Michele asked.

"You did fine," Dave said.

"I think you did great," Johnny said.

"Johnny," Dave said. "Take Mandy down now —slowly. When she's done swimming, I want her to practice again clearing her mask and finding and clearing her regulator."

"Is that necessary?" Johnny asked. "She seemed OK."

"Just do it," Dave ordered.

Dave removed Jean's and Michele's equipment before they got out of the pool. Jean's legs were covered with gooseflesh; she was shivering. More than anything she wanted to get up to her room and take a hot shower. But according to Dave they would soon have to prepare to drive out to the dive site. Apparently, it was good to dive when the sun was still high in the sky.

"Let's get some hot chocolate," Michele suggested. She glanced at Dave. "We have time for that, don't we?"

"If you hurry," he said.

"Shouldn't we wait for Mandy?" Jean asked.

"No," Michele said. "She could be in the pool another fifteen minutes."

They went over to the coffee shop area—it was more outside than inside—and got a seat in the sun. They had on their bathing suits and towels. That was the great thing about Hawaii; no one seemed to wear much more than a swimsuit. After a waitress came and took their orders, they sat silently and let the sun sink deep into them.

"Feels divine," Michele muttered. She looked over at Jean with her clear blue eyes. "Tell me about this boy on the plane."

"Mandy told you?"

"Yes. How come you didn't?"

"I didn't want to have to talk about it again," Jean said.

"You don't have to talk about it now," Michele said.

"All right. Thanks."

Michele seemed to be momentarily startled, but her cool demeanor instantly returned. She yawned and stretched her tan legs under the table. Jean reflected on how little she knew Michele. Even though they had talked frequently the last two months, the conversations had centered primarily on the trip. For the last four years at school they had moved in separate circles. Jean could count the things she knew about Michele on one hand: She was an excellent student; she never seemed upset under pressure; she was not shy; she had incredible self-confidence; and she didn't have a steady boy-friend. Other than that, Jean had no knowledge of Michele's likes or dislikes, her long-range goals, or her personal concerns. She didn't even know if Michele liked her or not.

Michele noticed her scrutiny. "What is it?" she asked.

"Nothing. I was just wondering if you had met Johnny and Dave the last time you were here."

Michele nodded slowly. "Dave. I met him briefly."

"How come you didn't take scuba lessons then?"

"I was too busy."

"Doing what?" Jean asked.

Michele grinned. "Screwing around."

Jean had to laugh. "Were you having sex with Dave when I got to the room?"

"That sounds like a personal question."

"You don't have to answer it if you don't want to."

"I don't mind. We were in the shower." Michele laughed to herself. "I suppose now you'll want to know how it was."

"Yeah. How was it?"

"Warm. Hot. The water was hot." Michele nodded to the packed beach. "There are a lot of boys here looking for girls. You shouldn't have any trouble."

"What makes you think I'm looking?"

"Mandy's already looking at Johnny, but he's looking at you." Michele brushed her long blond hair back. "There's lots of looking going on."

"I think it should be an interesting week," Jean said.

"So do I."

Their hot chocolate arrived five minutes later. By then, sitting in the sun, they were no longer cold. Michele ordered a Coke, too. Jean just stuck with the hot chocolate. She couldn't afford to waste anything.

CHAPTER

FIVE

They drove to the dive site in an old white van. Dave and Michele sat up front. Johnny crouched in back with the equipment—checking air pressure, tightening straps—and Mandy and Jean were in the middle. The mood was upbeat. Obviously, Dave and Johnny took beginners diving all the time, but they seemed to look forward to this dive as if it were their first. Jean wondered how it would be to live each day in the sun and water, with no tests to pass and no classes to attend. Just the thought of it was seductive.

Maybe I won't be getting on the plane to return home.

"How did you guys get into this business?" Jean asked Johnny.

"I grew up with Dave and his original partner," Johnny said.

"Is your partner still in the business with you?" Jean asked Dave.

Dave hesitated. "No, he's not."

His tone was instantly cool. Jean wondered if she was being too nosy. She changed the subject. "Will we see any sharks while we're diving?"

"Jean," Mandy said, more quiet than usual. "There are no sharks in Hawaii."

"You want to bet?" Johnny said. Then he laughed. "But the chances of seeing one are slim. Even if you do, they won't hurt you. The whole threat of sharks has been greatly exaggerated."

They reached the designated beach and parked the van. A small grass area separated the asphalt from the sand. Johnny and Dave piled the equipment onto the lawn.

"Now I have to explain a piece of equipment I haven't talked about," Dave said. He held up one of the black vests that was attached to a tank. "This is a buoyancy-control device. It's called a BC for short. You can put air into it, and you can take air out of it. Once you're in the water, you don't want to sink to the bottom or float to the surface. You want to be what is called neutrally buoyant. You won't have to learn how to work this device today. As we descend, Johnny and I will adjust your BCs. Let us do it. If you're floating to the surface, let us know with hand signals, and we'll add weight to your pouches. If you're stuck on the bottom, we'll add more air. Any questions? No? Good. Let's go over a few hand signals before we suit up. Remember, we won't be able to talk underwater."

Dave quickly gave them signals for when they were in trouble, when they needed help—basic things. Then they began to put on their equipment.

Dave made each of them wear a light skin suit vest. It was the only light thing they wore. Jean gasped as she put on the weight belt, and then the tank and the BC. The stuff weighed a ton!

"I feel like I'm going to fall over," Mandy complained, bent over as if she had the world on her back.

"You're not the only one," Michele said, for once sympathetic. She was breathing hard and Jean was breathing harder.

"I feel like I'll go straight to the bottom and not come up," Jean said. "Are you sure we need these weight belts?"

"Absolutely," Dave said. "Let's not stand here long. The weight will vanish the moment you're in water up to your necks." He pointed to the beach. "Those waves are no higher than two feet. But as you walk out with your equipment on, you can easily be knocked over by them. For that reason we'll walk out sideways, in a straight line and close together. I'll go first. Mandy will follow. Then Michele, Jean, and Johnny. You'll carry your fins in your right hands until I tell you to put them on. Put your masks on now. Is that clear?"

No one was going to argue. They just wanted to get in the water and get the weight off their backs. Together, they lumbered over the sand and into the sea. Jean had a moment of panic as the small waves began to lap at her legs. Although the ocean was much warmer than the pool, it seemed so much more dangerous. The idea that in a minute she would actually be breathing under its surface made her heart pound. She fought to calm herself, as she fought to maintain her balance.

I did it in the pool. I can do it here. I'm going to have fun. I had better have fun after all this trouble.

"Put your regulators in your mouths," Dave instructed when they were in water up to their knees. Initially the bottom was sand, but that changed suddenly. Jean stepped on something sharp and almost fell over.

Coral.

Jean focused through her mask, careful where she placed her bare feet. Soon, however, the bottom was nothing but coral, and there was nothing soft to put her feet on.

"Put your fins on," Dave said, doing likewise. "Use a buddy. Lean on each other for support."

Jean's buddy turned out to be Johnny, for which she was grateful. He was able to hold her perfectly steady in the surf while she got the fins on. With her regulator in her mouth, she couldn't speak. She was already breathing hard.

This is work.

Then Johnny took her hand and nodded for her to go down. She hesitated. There was white water all around them. Shouldn't they wait for a calm moment? Johnny wasn't letting her wait. He pulled her gently forward and down. Jean put her head in the water.

I'm going to choke!

She didn't choke. She discovered she could breathe perfectly with the regulator in her mouth, just as she had in the pool. But she was disoriented.

The surge of the waves tossed her first one way and then another, and it was sweeping up sand from the bottom. She could see less than two feet in front of her. Fortunately, Johnny had a firm hold on her hand. He pulled her forward, into deeper water, away from the shore and surf. Pressure squeezed against her eardrums. She reached up and cleared them, hearing a faint pop. She told herself to breathe, easily, deeply, the way Dave had instructed. She moved her legs up and down, rhythmically. She continued to clear her ears every few seconds.

Suddenly her vision cleared, and the surge became much less. Her disorientation vanished. What she saw in that moment literally took her breath away. She was surrounded by swimming fish and colored coral! She couldn't believe it; she could have fallen into a psychedelic dimension. She wanted to shout with joy. A wide-eyed purple fish stared at her from a couple of feet away. She smiled at him.

Water quickly seeped into her mask.

Damn.

She stopped smiling. Dave had warned them against too many facial expressions. She leaned over, pressed on the top of the mask, and slowly exhaled through her nose while tilting her head back. The water flowed out. Johnny squeezed her hand. He made a questioning OK sign. She made the OK sign back and nodded her head. She looked around. Dave was checking on Mandy and Michele. They both flashed OK signs. Then Jean raised her eyes to the surface. Once more she could hardly believe what she saw.

We're so deep.

The surface could have been over a hundred feet away. The bubbles streaming from their regulators seemed to take forever to reach the outside world. That was how Jean felt, as if she were in her own private world. She checked her depth gauge. They were only twenty-two feet below the surface.

They began to swim slowly about. Dave held Mandy's hand the whole time. Johnny stayed close to Jean and Michele but allowed them more freedom. The fish followed them. It must have been a common diving spot. When Dave clapped his hands together, the fish all rushed over. Jean assumed that the fish thought they were about to be fed. Alas, neither of the guys had brought food.

On the drive to the beach Johnny had said the visibility would be fifty feet, which Jean thought was about right. She couldn't get over how joyful the feeling of weightlessness was. And to think minutes before she had been sure she was going to collapse from the weight on her back. It was as if she were floating outside her body in a spiritual world. Johnny had adjusted her BC as soon as they were under, and she had no trouble maintaining neutral buoyancy. Mandy had troubles—she kept bobbing up. Johnny and Dave both had to add lead weights to the pouches in her BC. So much for lying about her weight. Michele swam along serenely, as if she were an old pro.

Dave was an expert guide. He pointed out numerous fish and unusual coral formations. There was one rather flat fish in particular that none of them saw until he shook it off the bottom; it blended in so well with the sand and the coral. Then there was a pointy urchin that Jean came within an inch of touching. Johnny barely stopped her, grabbing her hand and vigorously shaking his head.

The time passed quickly. After about thirty minutes, Dave stopped them and pointed to his air indicator. He wanted to know how much each of them had left. He had told them previous to the dive that he wanted to surface with at least five hundred psi left in their tanks, or about one sixth the original air supply. Jean saw hers was a little over a thousand, and conveyed the information to Dave by flashing all ten of her fingers. Michele had the same amount of air left. Unfortunately, Mandy was already down to five hundred psi. Dave signaled that they had to surface.

The guys watched them like hawks as they swam up. Jean had to make herself slow down repeatedly. She kept her gaze fixed on the surface. Dave had explained the importance of not coming up in front of a passing boat.

As they broke the surface, Johnny and Dave immediately reached over and inflated all their BCs. They bobbled on the surface without effort. They were about two hundred feet offshore. Mandy alone looked tired. Dave asked if she was OK.

"Yeah," she said heavily. "But my ears hurt."

"Did they hurt while you were under?" Dave asked.

"Yes."

"Why didn't you signal me?" Dave asked.

"I didn't want to slow the party down," Mandy said.

"Next time don't worry about that," Dave said. He looked toward the beach. "We've moved a bit south of where we entered, but I want to swim straight in. I suggest you swim with your mask in the water, using your snorkel instead of your regulator. Does everyone know how to do that? Good. All right, let's go."

Getting in—at least getting into the shallower water—was easy. But as soon as it was time to stand again, Jean groaned. The equipment felt even heavier than it had when they entered. Johnny reached out a helping hand.

"Get your fins off quickly," he advised. "Or you won't be able to walk."

She slipped out of them but toppled over as a wave hit her backside. She shot out her right arm to brace her fall and a stinging pain shot through her hand. She had scraped it on a jagged piece of coral. Blood dripped from her palm as she pulled it out of the water. Johnny held up his gloved hands. She had not noticed him wearing them before.

"That's why we wear these," he said. "I should have gotten some for you. Are you OK?"

"It's nothing. I just feel so heavy!"

He reached out and snapped her BC belts loose. "I'll take it," he said.

Another wave hit them, and they both almost went down this time. Dave was struggling with Mandy. Michele was already in.

"Are you sure you can handle it?" Jean asked, experiencing a twinge of guilt for dumping it on him. But it did feel so good to have the equipment off her back.

"I'm sure," Johnny said.

Free of the scuba gear, Jean was able to reach the beach in a matter of seconds. She crawled onto the sand and sat beside Michele, who was also huffing and puffing. "That was quite a workout," Jean said.

Michele grinned, her wet hair all over her face. "But it was worth it. Let's do it again tomorrow."

"Maybe," Jean said, thinking of how beautiful the underwater environment had been.

The rest of the group was in shortly afterward. Mandy collapsed on the sand, exhausted. Getting in and out consumed far more energy than the dive itself. Dave stood holding Mandy's gear as if it weighed a few ounces. He may have been strict, but he was patient. He let Mandy recover fully before he had them walk back to the van. Michele, alone of the girls, carried her own equipment.

They dried off quickly and climbed into the van. By then they had all caught their breath. The three girls talked excitedly about the things they had seen. The guys sat up front, chuckling at them. Michele was a wonder, she had so much energy. She wanted to know what they were going to do next.

"Eat," Mandy said.

"Take a nap," Jean said. It would be her third nap of the day, which was odd for her. But, of course, only the first one had been restful. The nightmare of Mike had ruined the second.

But it wasn't a dream.

That quick the memory of his sad expression cooled her enthusiasm.

"Why don't you take a nap at the hotel, Jean?" Johnny suggested. "Then we can all go out later and get something to eat." He glanced over his shoulder and flashed her his beach bum grin. "If that'd be OK."

Michele snorted with pleasure. "Sounds like a date to me."

"That would be fine with me," Jean said softly, wishing she could take more pleasure in the invitation. But she was still thinking of Mike, and the way he had choked as he had died, as if his lungs were full of cold blood.

"It would be fine with me, too," Mandy said flatly.

CHAPTER

SIX

Jean rested on top of the bed in the master bedroom. Her eyes were closed and her breathing was deep. She wore only her underwear. She listened to the gentle lulling of the waves and let her skin soak up the sensation of the warm ocean breeze as it wafted through the open door of the balcony. She was tired but not physically uncomfortable.

Still, she was troubled.

She was alone in the suite.

She fell asleep with trouble in her heart.

She dreamed. It seemed to start almost immediately. She didn't even know she was dreaming. It was almost as if she could have been another person, someone not quite alive.

She was lying on the bed where she had lain down not long before. Her eyes were open, however, and she was staring at the ceiling. Cool white light played on the flat dry plaster. It was the moon, dancing through the curtain that billowed wide and full with the wind. The wind had strength and power now. It wanted her to get up and move with it.

Jean sat up. She could hear a sound. Running water, maybe? The wind blew. It whispered in her mind. The sound of water was coming from the bathroom.

Jean stood. Except for the moonlight, the suite was dark. She stepped to the balcony and looked down. The pool lights were off. The entire beach was dark. In fact, there was no sign of another hotel on the entire shore. It was as if she were seeing the beach as it had been before human beings even walked on the planet.

The water continued to run in the bathroom. The wind blew in her face. Turn around, it seemed to say. Go this way, my way. I have something to show you.

Jean turned toward the bathroom. She took a step forward, then another. Her feet made no sound on the carpeted floor. There was only one noise, that of running water.

She noticed the bathroom light was on. She wasn't positive it had been on a moment ago. She was pretty sure it hadn't been. She wondered if the wind had turned it on.

So that she could see.

Jean entered the bathroom. The shower curtain was pulled over. She couldn't see directly into the bathtub. To do that she would have to cross the floor and pull back the curtain. But suddenly it seemed as if that would take too much effort. The bathroom was not big. It was far smaller than the bedroom she had just traversed. Yet she felt if she started to cross the neatly laid tiles, it might be hours before she reached the other end. The tiles were lined up in such straight lines. As she stared at them, it was as if she saw them through the eyes of an insect crawling along the floor. Endless lines before her, and always the possibility of being crushed before the journey could be completed.

The wind blew again, cold at her back. It sent a chill through the length of her body. It prodded her forward. There is no comfort on the outside, it seemed to say. You will have to go forward, toward the running water, and see from where it springs.

Jean stepped across the bathroom.

She pulled the curtain aside.

Clean sparkling water poured out of the faucet.

But the bathtub was full of blood.

Faint wisps of steam rose from its surface. Water ran into the tub of blood, yet the red liquid remained undisturbed, calm and smooth, so smooth Jean knew she could see her reflection in it if she was willing to lean over and peer into its depths.

Yes, do that, the wind at Jean's back said to her in a voice that was not her own, a soft voice that was neither male or female. A sad voice that was somehow both lost and still undiscovered. Just find your own reflection in the blood, and things will become clear.

But Jean did not want to look. She feared she might slip forward, and then her face would fall in the blood, and it would get in her eyes, and if she tried to take a breath, she would choke on the warm red viscous liquid. She knew this was a possibility. She felt, as she stared at the tub, that someone had already gone before her, and stared into its depths, and fallen, and been lost. She thought she might be staring at the blood that person had left behind.

Jean did decide to do one thing, however. She wanted to turn the water off. The sound of it was growing louder, unbearably loud. It filled her ears, crowding out what few thoughts she did have. It poured steadily into the tub, yet as she listened carefully, she could make out a subtle rhythm to the steady pounding. It slowly pulsated. Jean glanced back into the suite and watched as the curtains billowed in the moonlight. They seemed to move to the same rhythm as the running water.

Jean reached out for the faucet and turned it.

But suddenly a gust of red steam rose up from the bloody tub. It hit her in the face. It smelled of death, of morbid decay, and it made her feel faint. She shot out her right hand to brace herself against the wall. She knew somehow, from a part of her that seemed distant, that she had earlier cut this same hand. She felt that it was still cut and bleeding, and as it contacted the tiles, she was not entirely surprised that it slipped and lost its grip. As her face plummeted toward the bloody bathtub, she let out a scream of absolute horror.

She let it out, but no sound followed.

Her breath was cut off. She was choking.

She kept falling toward the tub. But she never hit it. On the other side, though, coming up from the depths of the blood, she saw something. A face. Choking as she was choking. The face was of a young man she recognized.

It was Mike. Mike Clyde in the bath of blood.

The dead boy.

But I am not dead.

Jean screamed.

Jean bolted upright in the bed, her eyes open. It took her a moment to realize where she was.

Hawaii. Paradise.

"What a nightmare," she whispered.

The evening sky shone outside the balcony door. The sun was still up, but it wouldn't be for long. A hard wind flapped the curtains, making an odd beating sound. Jean stood up from the bed and closed the door. She was surprised that she was soaked with sweat.

And to hear the water in the bathtub running.

"Hello," she called, moving to the bathroom door. "Is that you, Michele? Mandy? Who's in there?"

No one answered. That was no big deal. They probably couldn't hear her. Or maybe someone had started the bath running and left without turning it off. It was possible to enter the suite bathroom through a door in the living room without going through the bedroom where she had been sleeping.

It's no big deal. Why don't you just open the bathroom door and look for yourself?

The obvious answer was because she was scared. She had just had a nightmare about a bloody tub, and a bathtub wasn't what she wanted to look at. At least, not until she was sure she was a hundred percent awake. Of course, she already knew she was awake. When she pinched her arm it hurt. That was the acid test. So why not open the door and see what the big deal was?

Because I've never had a nightmare like that in my life.

It was true. Everything about it—the sounds, the colors—had been as vivid as the shapes and hues of coral seen underwater. The dream had been more like a slow parade of still pictures than like the images of a weary subconscious.

"Mandy?" Jean called. "Michele?"

Silence. An old friend. Except at times like this, when it could be the worst of enemies. Jean put her hand on the doorknob. It was cool to the touch. It shouldn't have been. This was Hawaii. Everything was supposed to be warm and alive.

You're being ridiculous. It's cool because it's metal. There isn't a dead boy waiting on the other side of the door in the bathtub.

"That's true," Jean whispered.

She opened the door.

Clean water ran freely into the tub.

But the bath was full of red liquid.

Earlier, just after they had arrived back at their hotel room, Michele had called room service and asked them to send up a plate of french fries. Apparently, Michele was a fry addict, who also needed daily doses of catsup. She had told the people at room service also to bring up a bottle of

71

premium Heinz. The food had arrived shortly before Jean stretched out for her nap, and Michele and Mandy left to go lie by the pool.

Michele had some weird habits, after all. She did not simply dip her fries in a spot of catsup and eat them. She stuck each fry directly *into* the catsup bottle. The whole time she had eaten the fries, she pranced about the suite with her bottle in her hand. She enjoyed grossing them out.

Jean took a step closer to the bathtub.

It's not blood. It's not blood!

At one time or another Michele must have gone into the bathroom and set the bottle on the ledge of the tub. It was probably she who had turned on the water in the tub. In either case, the bottle must have fallen into the tub and broken. That was the only explanation.

Jean stopped and leaned over the tub.

There was no blood. There was only broken glass and catsup.

She sighed with relief for more than one reason. She was glad the overflow hole was larger than most and took off all the excess water.

Then she thought what a strange coincidence it was that the tub had been filled with red, just as it had been in her dream. She had to lie down again. But she was careful not to sleep. No more dreams.

CHAPTER

SEVEN

From the start the mathematics of the date were not promising. There were two guys and three girls. Jean could see trouble coming as she climbed in the blue Mustang. The car was not so nice as their own rental, but she thought it would have been rude to say so. Dave and Michele sat in the front. Johnny, Mandy, and Jean were in the back. Jean got to sit next to Johnny. She didn't plan it that way, but it seemed as if Johnny had.

The idea was to go to dinner and then out to a disco. Dave drove toward the group of hotels a mile south of their own. He knew a place, he said, that was right on the water and served great seafood.

The restaurant was crowded, and they had to wait. Mandy appeared to be in an upbeat mood. She chatted loudly, asking the guys every conceivable question about the island. But Jean could see she was trying too hard. At first Dave and Johnny answered each of her questions, but then they, too, sensed that she was just trying to make conversation. Dave started to look around when she was talking, or else he talked right through her to Michele. Jean felt bad. Johnny remained quiet, and by the time they were seated, Mandy had gotten the point and spoke little.

Their table was outside on a balcony, right beside the beach. They could see the gentle waves rolling up in the serene moonlight. Tall torches burned like ancient sentinels up and down the shoreline.

"Talk about atmosphere," Jean said as they were seated. The night was warm, and she had worn shorts and a light top, as the rest of them had. Dave was pleased by her comment and flashed her a rare smile.

"We only go here when we're feeling rich," he said.

"And that isn't too often," Johnny said.

"Has business been slow?" Jean asked.

"It's fine this week," Dave said. "But that's because it's Easter vacation. Otherwise, it's been hard. There are dozens of boats fighting for each tourist who wants to go out on the water."

"Do you mainly take people scuba diving?" Jean asked.

"Or snorkeling," Johnny said. "Or whale watching. If they've got cash, we let them do what they want. Tomorrow we're not working at the hotel. We're going out to Lanai."

"Yeah, we've got a full boat," Dave said quickly. "We should make some money."

Their waiter came and took their orders. He was a goofy teenager, very pleasant. They all had fish, except Mandy, who wanted a salad. It was another sign of trouble. Now she was dieting, Jean thought, so she'd look better for the guys. Jean ordered *mahimahi*, which she had read about in her travel book. Michele, of course, ordered something none of them could pronounce.

The food came and was delicious. Johnny began to tell stories about different boating expeditions. He gestured out to Lanai, which was now only a low moonlit mound far out in the sea.

"The water looks calm tonight," Johnny said. "But sometimes you get big swells between the islands. Once the three of us were out in the boat with a bunch of tourists, and twenty-foot swells came up. The weather reports gave us no warning. Those poor people. They were green by the time we got back to the harbor. But they were happy to be alive."

The three of us . . . He's referring to their old partner. I won't ask about him again, not with Dave around.

"How big is your boat?" Jean asked.

"It's a thirty-five-foot cabin cruiser," Johnny said.

Jean was impressed. "That's big. It must be neat knowing you can jump in it and visit any of the islands. I've always dreamed of owning a boat."

Dave snorted. "So do we. The bank owns ours."

Johnny nodded. "We pay them every month, or we try to."

There was a pause in the conversation. Jean was getting the idea that the boys' job in paradise was harder and more of a struggle than it appeared to be. Michele glanced first at the two guys and then lowered her eyes and spoke in an odd tone that was teasing and cautious at the same time.

"Maybe what you need is to search for sunken treasure," she said, lifting her chin.

Dave stared out at the water. "We've tried that already."

"Really?" Jean asked.

"It's a long story," Johnny said.

"I like stories," Michele said.

"You know most of it now," Dave said coolly.

Another sensitive point. Interesting.

"I don't know it," Mandy said.

Johnny picked up his water and sipped it slowly. He spoke softer than usual. "There was a yacht a year ago called the *Moonflower,* a sixty-foot beauty. It was owned by a very wealthy family on Maui, and they often took important visitors out on it. They had an experienced captain, but like us, they got caught once in a storm with big swells. I don't know how it could happen to a boat that big, but it capsized. A huge wave probably washed over it at the wrong angle. Both the owners and a couple of their guests drowned. The rest managed to escape in a lifeboat. The yacht sank."

"And it was never found?" Jean asked.

"It was found," Johnny said. "It sank only a quarter mile off Lanai. But before it went down, the surf raked it over the coral around the island. It was split from bow to stern. Everything that was in it was spilled over the ocean floor."

"What was in it?" Jean asked.

"Treasure," Johnny said.

"Maybe," Dave interrupted, obviously not pleased with the telling of the tale. "There were stories that the owners had a safe on board."

"Why would anyone keep valuables aboard a yacht?" Jean asked.

"That's what I said," Dave said. "I think the stories are rubbish."

Now Johnny was displeased. "There were a lot of rich people on that yacht when it got torn apart," he said. "Even if there was no safe, a lot of money was left lying on the bottom."

Michele nodded. "Wallets. Purses. Jewelry."

"Did they recover the bodies of all those who drowned?" Jean asked.

"Yes," Dave said.

Jean hesitated. "You didn't know anyone who was on the boat?"

"No," Johnny said, meeting Dave's eyes.

"We don't know any rich people," Dave said, sounding disgusted.

"Did you guys go hunting for the treasure?" Mandy asked.

"I didn't," Dave said.

"Many scuba divers on the island searched the area," Johnny said. "Certain small articles were found, as Michele said. Watches, necklaces— nothing of extraordinary value."

"Did you search?" Jean asked Johnny. He was uncomfortable with the question.

"A little" was all he said.

* * *

They finished their meal and prepared to leave. The guys paid the bill. Jean was happy they did. She was still counting her pennies—there was a long week to go, after all. But she did feel guilty for not chipping in. She was used to being self-sufficient.

It was time to dance to loud music, but they had hardly entered the disco when Mandy said that she wanted to return to the hotel because she wasn't feeling well. She wasn't trying to put anyone out. She said she would just catch a cab. But it was obvious she wasn't happy. No one said much at her announcement, but Jean pulled her aside as she started to leave.

"Are you really sick?" Jean asked her, standing just outside the disco doorway. Behind them the music throbbed.

"I'm just tired," Mandy said, staring at the ground.

"Cut the crap. Tell me the problem."

Mandy raised her head and forced a chuckle. "The problem is, I'm not as cute as you and Michele. But since we can't fix that tonight, I may as well go back and get my beauty sleep so that I look better tomorrow."

"Mandy."

"What?"

"We're on vacation," Jean said. "We're here to have fun. We are having fun. Don't start feeling sorry for yourself."

"I'm not. Well, maybe I am. Damn." Mandy sniffed. She reached for a tissue in her purse. Jean

78

put an arm around her. Mandy quickly muffled her sniffles. She spoke as if she was trying to convince herself of what she was saying. "He just prefers you to me, that's all. I understand. It's OK. I'll find someone else."

"Are you talking about Johnny?" Jean asked. It was a stupid question.

"I'm not talking about Batman," Mandy said. "I told you I liked him. But don't feel guilty. I'm glad he likes you." She wiped at her eyes again and smiled. "I'm happy, I really am. But I want to go now. You know what a klutz I am on the dance floor. Please just let me go."

Jean hugged her. "I can go back with you?"

"Absolutely not." Mandy hugged her in return, then let go of her and turned away. But she paused midstep, speaking over her shoulder. "Don't tell me if you kiss him."

"I won't. I promise."

Mandy glanced back at her. She was unhappy, but she still had her sense of humor. "You won't what? What is the promise?"

Jean laughed. "You know me too well. Get home. Get some rest."

Mandy left. Jean went back inside and let the music take over. Michele was already on the floor with Dave. She was a great dancer, with her long legs, but Jean knew she could show her a move or two. She often turned the music up loud when her parents weren't home, and let it all hang out. She knew how to rock. She let Johnny pull her onto the floor. He laughed as he began to move with her.

"Hey, you're good," he said.

She smiled. He was a cutey. "I'm the best," she said.

They danced for an hour straight, had a couple of Cokes, then danced some more. It was Johnny who got tired first. He finally pulled her off the floor. He had to yell to be heard. Her ears were ringing.

"Do you want to go for a walk on the beach?" he asked.

She nodded. "Sure!"

They told Dave and Michele they'd catch them later. Walking from the disco to the beach was like stepping into another world. It was almost midnight; there was no one on the sand. And it was so silent. They headed north, away from the hotels, with their shoes off, letting the gentle surf rush over their feet. The moonlight glistened on the water and in Johnny's eyes. He reached over and took her hand.

"Are you having fun?" he asked.

"Oh, yeah. It's so neat here."

They walked farther, making small talk, and then sat down in the sand just out of reach of the waves. In the distance the small island of Lanai was clearly visible. She pointed to it.

"What's it like scuba diving out there?" she asked.

"It makes the dive this afternoon look like nothing," Johnny said. "The visibility out there's usually over a hundred feet and the coral is indescribable. There's this one place called the cathedrals. The sun shines through these openings in stone, sending out bizarre shafts of light." He gestured to the moon. "You can go diving there at night when the moon is full, and it's even more beautiful. All kinds of strange fish come out then."

"When the moon is full, it lights up the water at night. You can see the dark fish. You can see the caves of colored coral. The fish swim in the caves, and the tide rushes out. When the time is right, the water rushes through the moonlight to the end of the cave."

How had Mike known about the fish that came out at night? He must have read it in a book.

Why did the catsup bottle fall in the tub while I was dreaming about blood?

Of course the questions weren't related.

The only thing they had in common was Mike. Poor Mike.

Jean had later asked Michele about the catsup bottle. Michele had admitted leaving it near the bathtub. But she swore she had left it far from the edge. She couldn't understand how it had fallen and broken.

"It's like someone came in and knocked it over," Michele had complained as she helped Jean clean up the mess.

"Jean?" Johnny asked.

"Huh?"

"You spaced out there for a moment. What were you thinking about?"

She started to tell him about Mike and her nightmare, but something stopped her. Perhaps it was because the night was so serene, she didn't

81

want to spoil the mood. Also, what did she have to say? That a nice boy she had met on the plane had died after telling her about a nighttime dive site? A boy who had never even been in the ocean, never mind to Hawaii? Johnny would think she was crazy.

"I was just thinking about the *Moonflower*," she lied. "That was an interesting story. How much did you search the area for treasure?"

"A lot. Ringo and I were out there almost every day right after the wreck."

"Ringo's your old partner?"

"Yeah," Johnny said.

"Dave doesn't like to talk about him?"

Johnny paused, playing with the sand beside his bent knees. "That's because Ringo's dead."

"What?" She was shocked. "How did he die?"

Johnny lowered his head. "We don't know exactly. They never found his body. But he died on a dive off Lanai, and it was at night, in the vicinity of where the *Moonflower* was lost."

"How do you know that if his body was never found?"

"Because our boat was anchored out there," Johnny said.

"Was anyone else aboard the boat?"

"No. If there had been, we'd know a lot more about what happened."

"Is there any chance he could still be alive?" Jean asked.

"I guess if Ringo had wanted to disappear, he could have arranged the situation. But he would never have done that. Ringo was the boss behind our business. He got us most of our clients. He was a real hustler. That's why we've had to struggle so hard since he's been gone." Johnny opened his hand and let the sand slip away. "No, he's dead. There's no doubt in my mind."

"Dave must have taken the loss of Ringo hard, the way he freezes up whenever his name is mentioned."

"Oh, yeah. So did I. I grew up with Ringo." Johnny's gaze was fixed out over the calm sea. "You know, he was always a reckless diver. When we were looking for stuff from the *Moonflower*, he made far too many repetitive dives."

"What does that mean?" Jean asked.

"When you dive again before all the nitrogen has been flushed out of your system, it's called a repetitive dive. Even during the dive you made today, the nitrogen level in your blood rose. But it was a shallow dive. The effect was small. The deeper you go, and the longer you stay down, the more nitrogen you build up. Then if you make another dive soon after that, and then another, you risk getting the bends." Johnny shook his head. "One day while we were searching for the *Moonflower* money, Ringo made five dives close to one another. He got the beginning symptoms of the bends. I told him he was crazy."

"So you think he got the bends and drowned?" Jean asked.

"That's what I think."

"Does Dave think something else?"

"I'm not sure what Dave thinks. He won't talk about it."

"Why would Ringo have gone diving at night?" Jean asked. "I would imagine it would be harder to spot things in the dark."

"It is. But you have to realize Ringo died only a week after the *Moonflower* went down. The waters off Lanai were crawling with divers. If Ringo had gotten a lead on where some things were, he might have wanted to go back at night so no one could see what he'd found and where he found it. You see, we were all looking for stuff that didn't belong to us. The rich couple that owned the *Moonflower* had plenty of family that were still alive. It was understood that if you found anything, you would have to sell it under the table."

"But that would have been like stealing," she said.

Johnny smiled at her. "The ocean's a big place. If anyone can find anything valuable in it, they deserve it." He met her eyes with an odd, almost nasty, look. "Finder's keepers, as they say."

She chuckled. "I hope you don't feel that way about the girls you meet."

His grin widened and became as wicked as the rest of his expression. "I didn't find you in the ocean, but by the pool. That's different."

"How so?" she asked.

He put his hand on her left shoulder. "I don't get to keep you for good."

"Oh."

He leaned over and put his other hand on her

84

right shoulder. His touch was warm; the warmth traveled right through her skin to her bones. She knew he was about to kiss her, and she wasn't sure what she was going to do, only that she probably wasn't going to stop him.

Which means you're going to kiss him back. Don't fool yourself.

"I only get to keep you for the week," he said, his face mere inches from hers now. She could feel the warmth of his breath on her cheek. His messy blond hair hung down into his face, and his eyes glistened in the moonlight. He swung his right leg around to the far side of her. He had her cornered.

"Do I have any say in this?" she asked.

"Sure. You could stay an extra week." He leaned closer, pressing the side of his head against hers. His arms went around her. He spoke in her ear. "You could stay as long as you'd like." He gently pulled her head back so that he could see her face. "What do you say, Jean?"

What was the question?

"Yes," she whispered.

He closed his eyes and leaned over. She closed her eyes and puckered up.

A beeper in his pocket went off.

"Damn," he muttered. He let go of her and sat back a couple of feet. He dug the beeper out of his pocket and turned it off. "Excuse me," he said.

She laughed. "You don't look like the sort to have one of those."

He nodded. "It's necessary in our business. Clients call our machine and want to go out on the boat at a moment's notice. Our message says we'll call them back within ten minutes."

"Does that mean we have to find a phone?"

"Yeah, right away." Johnny stood up and brushed the sand off his shorts. As he offered her his hand, he looked disappointed. "I wish it was Dave's week to carry the beeper."

She hopped up, and Johnny helped her brush off her bottom, of all spots. It felt kind of good. At least he wasn't a religious fanatic or a hypochondriac.

"You switch off, week to week?" she asked.

"Yeah. When Ringo was alive, he always carried it."

"You do miss him," she said sympathetically.

"Yeah."

"Johnny? How old was Ringo?"

"Twenty-three. Why?"

"I don't know. For some reason I just thought he was younger."

Like Mike's age.

Another ridiculous thought. The only thing that those guys had in common was that they were both dead. She had never dreamed about Ringo.

They returned to the disco, holding hands the whole way. Johnny found a phone booth outside. He called a few yards away while she leaned against the disco wall. He was on the phone only a minute before he rushed back to her.

"There's a problem," he said, concerned.

"What is it?"

"Let me tell you in a second. I've got to see if I can take the car. Stay here. Let me talk to Dave."

Johnny was inside a short time. When he returned, he was still as anxious to get going. She chased after him.

"Dave's going to take a cab with Michele back to your hotel," he said. "We can take the car."

"That means Dave must be spending the night," she said.

"Does that bother you?"

"No. It's just going to be crowded in the suite." They turned in the direction of the parking lot. "Now tell me what the emergency is?"

Johnny looked more uncomfortable. "It's my mother."

"What's wrong with her? Is she sick?"

"No. Yes. It's complicated."

"You don't have to talk about it if you don't want to."

He stopped and jammed his hands in his pockets and stared at the ground. "I never have anyone I can talk to about it," he said.

She touched his arm. "What is it, Johnny?"

He looked up. "She's an alcoholic."

"Is she bad?"

"Bad enough."

"What's happened to her tonight?" she asked.

"Our neighbor called. He says she fell down and cut her head open. His wife already took her to the hospital, so I'm sure she'll be all right. I should take you back to the hotel before going home."

"No. I want to go with you." A wave of warmth for him swept over her. Talking about his mother was obviously difficult for him. She appreciated the fact that he trusted her enough to tell her the truth. She moved closer to him. "That is, if you want me there. I don't want to get in your way."

"You're a nice person. Did anyone ever tell you that?"

"Never," she joked. "Everybody I know thinks I'm a complete bitch."

"You know the wrong kind of people."

"No." She poked him lightly in the stomach and jumped back. "I know you."

They climbed in the car and drove south along the coast, heading toward the Maui city of Lahaina —tiny by California standards, but it was the largest city on the island. Jean had passed through it on the drive in from the airport. Johnny explained as they drove that he and his mom had lived in a Lahaina condo since he was a kid. He didn't mention his father, and Jean didn't pry.

Johnny may have been willing to talk about his mom, but when they reached his place he asked if it would be OK if she stayed in the car. Jean understood how tricky family matters could be.

"No problem," she said. "As long as no one steals me while you're gone."

"This neighborhood is pretty safe." He glanced around. "But keep the door locked until I get back."

She watched as he jogged up a flight of stairs and disappeared into a lit condo. The curtains were drawn so she couldn't see what was going on inside. He was gone for quite a while.

All of a sudden she had to go to the bathroom.

She had drunk one soda too many at the disco. She tried waiting it out, hoping he'd reappear any second, but he didn't, and she began to feel *real* uncomfortable. Her bladder had always been on the small side. She literally felt as if she would pee in her shorts any second. She got out of the car and searched the street. They were in a residential area. She couldn't imagine how far the nearest gas station was. She couldn't even see a good row of bushes to go behind.

I've got to knock on his door. Johnny will understand.

Jean walked up the flight of stairs. She hesitated before she rang the bell. She could hear them talking inside, and it didn't sound as if they were enjoying pleasant conversation. But she had no choice. She was squirming in her sandals. She pushed the tiny metal button beside the door. *Ding-dong.*

Johnny answered the door. At first he looked put out, but he quickly regained his manners. "I'm sorry," he said. "I was just coming down."

"I have to use your restroom. Would that be OK?"

He glanced over his shoulder. A middle-aged woman hovered in the background. Jean could only catch a glimpse of her. "Sure," Johnny said, stepping aside. "Come in."

The woman didn't look like a mother. Nor did she look particularly drunk. She had on a short, tight black skirt. Her purple cotton sweater was twenty years too young for her. But it was her makeup that was the worst—there was way too much of it. She smiled when she saw Jean, but with a hard line of lipstick. It was clear to Jean that she was walking in on the middle of an argument.

She was supposed to have split her head open. Where are the blood and bandages?

As Jean studied her closer, however, she noticed that the woman's left eye was swollen almost shut. She spotted a plastic bag filled with ice on the coffee table. The woman noticed where she was looking.

"Is this your friend, Johnny?" the woman asked. "She doesn't look very old."

"I'm eighteen," Jean said stiffly.

"The restroom's at the end of the hall on the left," Johnny said quickly.

"Aren't you going to introduce me to your new squeeze?" the woman asked.

"Mom," Johnny said, exasperated. "Don't."

"My name's Jean," Jean said. She stepped across the room and offered her hand. "I'm pleased to meet you."

"I'm Carol." They shook hands. The woman regarded her critically. "You have to use the head? Did you drink too much tonight?"

"I don't drink," Jean said. She had had only a few beers in her life. Still she noticed no outward sign of drunkenness in the mother.

"Just use the restroom, then we should go," Johnny said

His mother glared at him. "What's the matter? Are you ashamed of me?"

"We can talk later," Johnny muttered.

The woman reached for her ice bag and applied it

to her eye. "That's fine with me. My head feels like it's going to explode."

Jean left the living room and used the bathroom. When she was done, Johnny already had the front door open. "You're not going out?" he asked his mother.

"No," she said flatly, sitting down and turning on the TV, her ice bag still in her hand. "Nice meeting you, Jean."

It was a joy and an honor.

"Same here," Jean said.

When they were in the car, heading back to the hotel, Jean asked Johnny what the deal was. He shrugged.

"Obviously, my neighbor exaggerated," he said. "She just fell down and banged her head."

"She didn't seem drunk."

"That's the thing with alcoholics. They can down a whole bottle and still appear sober."

"I'm sorry I came in when I did. I just can't hold my Cokes."

"It wasn't your fault," he said, but his mood remained gloomy for the rest of the drive. Only when he was dropping her off at the front of the hotel did his spirits pick up. "Would you like me to walk you up to your room?" he asked.

"It's not necessary." She opened the car door, smiling at him. "I had a great time tonight."

"What are you doing tomorrow?"

"I don't know. I'll have to see what the girls want to do."

"Michele might be going on the boat with us," Johnny said.

"But Dave made it clear at dinner there was no room." She paused. "But I guess there's always room for someone who looks like Michele."

"There's room for you, too. If you want to come."

She had been hoping for an invitation. Each time she had looked out at Lanai, and heard about it, she had been filled with a longing to go there.

Dark fish. Colored caves of coral.

"Won't it be too crowded?" she asked.

"It will be crowded," he admitted.

"Have you asked Dave if it would be OK?"

"No."

"Will he mind?"

Johnny thought a moment. "Probably. But he's bringing Michele."

"You're sure?" she asked.

"Yeah. He told me."

Michele hadn't told them. Jean resented her making plans without consulting them. "I couldn't go unless Mandy was allowed to come," she said. "It wouldn't be fair to leave her out."

"I doubt Dave would go for that. One extra person is fine. Two is stretching it. Three would probably be out of the question. You have to understand that the people we take out have paid. We provide them with lunch and scuba or snorkeling instructions. People don't like being on a boat that's too crowded. They can't sunbathe, and they won't give us referrals if they're not satisfied." Johnny sighed. "That's how Ringo got most of our business—from referrals. He would psych clients into getting all their friends to call us."

"Are you guys having financial troubles?" Jean asked.

"Not yet. But we're getting there. We may have to sell the boat and get something smaller. But it would probably be a mistake. People wouldn't have as much fun, and business would only get worse."

"If Mandy and I came we could pay," Jean said, not sure how much such a trip would cost. Johnny shook his head.

"No way," he said. "I feel bad I charged you for the scuba lesson today."

"But that's your job. The hotel required you to charge us."

He finally grinned, and it was good to see again. Talk about the financial side of his business obviously dragged him down.

"I guess I'm feeling guilty about mixing business and pleasure," he said.

"Don't feel guilty." She leaned over and gave him a quick kiss on the cheek. A bellhop was watching them; she didn't want to get any more physical. She began to get out of the car. He grabbed her arm.

"Come tomorrow to the boat," he said. "Bring Mandy. People often cancel. We'll work something out."

"Are you sure?"

He leaned over and kissed her briefly on the lips. "Sure I'm sure."

I'm sure, too. God, that was a kiss. Short but sweet.

"Where do we go in the morning?" she asked, feeling breathless.

He let go of her arm. "Dave's probably with Michele. In either case, Michele knows where we're docked. Our boat's called the *Windspeed.*"

"Nice name. I like *Moonflower,* too." She stood outside the car now, leaning in. The bellhop was definitely watching them out the corner of his eye. She glanced out to sea. Something was troubling her. It took her a moment to clarify. "Was Michele here when the *Moonflower* sank?" she asked.

"She came a few days after it went down. Why?"

"She was here when Ringo died?"

"Yes."

"Has she scuba dived before?" Jean asked.

Johnny shrugged. "She's not certified, but I think she's taken an introductory course."

"That's weird. I asked her if she had, and she denied ever having scuba dived before."

"I could be wrong. What's the matter?"

"Nothing." She smiled quickly. "I guess I'll be seeing you in the morning." She glanced at her watch. It was past two. "God, what time does the boat leave?"

"Not till eight."

"Eight's early," she complained.

"We sometimes leave at six." He laughed at her. "Just think how tired Michele and Dave are going to be."

She laughed. "I see your point. Good night, Johnny. Thanks again."

"Sweet dreams, Jean."

She watched him drive away before heading for the elevator. He was a nice guy. He was the first nice guy she had met in a long time. Plus he liked her, which meant he had good taste. Already it was beginning to bother her that she would have to say goodbye to him the next Sunday.

Inside the suite she found Mandy fast asleep on the foldout bed in the living room. She could hear someone snoring through the door in the master bedroom, but it didn't sound like Michele. She didn't care. She was tired and could sleep anywhere. She made a quick stop in the bathroom and then stripped down to her underwear and climbed in bed beside Mandy. It was big enough for two of them. Mandy hardly stirred as she shifted over to make room for her. The breeze came through the open balcony door, warm and soft and faintly scented. Jean once again vowed to herself that she wouldn't go out to Lanai unless Mandy was allowed to come along. No matter how tempted she was.

"Sweet dreams, Jean."

She hoped they were sweet.

But they weren't.

The place was dark and wet. Far below, where living creatures ordinarily breathed. The moon shone through the many feet of water above her, but seen from that great depth, it looked distorted and squashed. Fish, swimming in slow motion around her, had eyes as big as pennies and lips that looked as cold and hard as stone. She had on scuba equipment and was diving where humans were not welcome. The black mouth of a cave waited in front of her.

She went inside.

The current lifted her forward as she moved in deeper. Through cracks in the ceiling of the cave, shafts of moonlight stabbed through. She was afraid, yet the surge held her as the wind had held her during her walk to the bloody bathroom. She could remember that incident even now, but she could not remember that it had been a dream. Everything seemed more real to her than her own breath, which dragged in and out of her lungs like winter frost. The water was supposed to be warm even in tropical depths, but the moonlight made it cold.

Then she came to Mike.

She had known he would be waiting for her. All her unwelcome visions, she also knew, were from Mike, who was calling to her from beyond his grave. She knew he was dead, and even when he held out his hand for her to stop in the middle of the black coral cave, she didn't panic. He had on scuba gear as she did. Bubbles rose all around his head. He may have been dead, but he was breathing. Somehow that made him far less fearsome.

He gestured for her to follow him, departing from the straight course of the cave down a narrow crevasse that was more of a tunnel than a cave. It was a one-way trip, this particular passageway; it suddenly dead-ended in a wall of jagged rock. Impaled in the rocks, at an angle that would have been painful had there been anything left alive to care, was a skeleton.

Mike shone a light on the remains, and the bony teeth and the empty eye sockets glowed faint phosphorescent green. They seemed to glow from the *inside.* As Jean gazed in wonder, she noticed that a large portion of the light was spilling out a small hole on the side of the skeleton's skull. Mike pointed to it. This, he appeared to be saying, was one of the reasons he had brought her to this place.

But it wasn't his only reason. Mike pulled a white balloon from his BC pouch and took his regulator from his mouth and attached it to the opening of the balloon. Jean reached forward to stop him. Without air, she thought, he would die. He would die *again* in front of her. She remembered then how he had died on the plane. She began to panic. She couldn't go through that again.

But he wouldn't stop. He wouldn't allow himself to breathe. His face became twisted in a mask of grotesque pain, but still he fed the white balloon with his only supply of air. And as it grew, it took on the shape of a heart. A pulsating heart, but still white and filled now with icy breath. It grew and grew, and she thought Mike should have been satisfied that it was big enough and taken his air back.

But he wasn't satisfied. Jean finally understood what he intended to do. She began to back away. He was going to pop the balloon. He was going to let his heart burst. And when he did, the pain that showed on his face would go away, but then so would everything else: the cave, the skeleton, the light. All would be dark, and she would be alone in the dark.

"Stop!" she shrieked at him through her regulator.

He stopped, but only for a moment. As the

balloon reached its expansive limit, he paused and studied her. For a moment the pain on his face vanished and was replaced with sorrow. He whispered silent words.

"You're sitting in my seat."

Then he coughed. And the balloon exploded.

"No!" Jean screamed soundlessly.

The darkness came.

"No!" Jean screamed.

She came to with strong hands pulling on her. A turquoise pool and an unlit beach swam in her vision. She was upside down! She was falling!

"What the hell are you doing?" a rough voice sounded in her ears. The same strong hands pulled her upright. The night stopped its dangerous dance. Jean looked around. She was on the balcony. Dave stood before her in his underwear. He let go of her panties, which was where he had grabbed her.

"What happened?" she gasped.

"I rolled over in bed and saw you stumbling around out here," he growled. "You were leaning over the edge of the balcony." He held his index fingers an inch apart. "You came that close to going over the side."

She felt like fainting. "Oh, God," she whispered.

"Do you usually sleepwalk?" Dave asked. "If you do, you'd better get a room on the ground floor right now."

She took a long, deep breath and let it out slowly. Her heart was racing. "I have never gone sleepwalking in my life," she said.

He looked her up and down, and for the first time

she realized she was only in a T-shirt and panties. "You're a funny girl, Jean," he said.

"Why do you say that?"

"There's just something about you. I don't know what it is."

She remembered her dream. Her dream that hadn't been a dream. How could she have had two such visions in the same day.

Visions?

They were like that. They were trying to lead her to something.

"It's like I'm haunted, isn't it?" she asked softly.

"Yeah, now that you mention it. What gives?"

Nothing gives. Can't you see that's my problem? I have no idea what's going on. Maybe if I'd fallen off the balcony, things would make sense. Then Mike and I could have had a one-on-one conversation.

"I don't know," she said, answering his question. "Thanks for saving my life." She turned away. "I'll lock the balcony door before I go back to bed. You won't have to worry about me anymore."

"I hope not," Dave said.

CHAPTER

EIGHT

There was one cancellation for the trip to Lanai aboard the *Windspeed*. Dave confirmed it as he moved among his clients with an open notebook in his hands. Still, he was not pleased. He scowled as he glanced at Jean and Mandy sitting together on the dock in the sweet Hawaiian morning air.

"It's going to be too crowded," he said.

"We don't have to go," Jean said.

"I don't have to go," Mandy said.

"Don't say that." Jean silenced her.

"I don't want to be rude, but it would probably be better if you didn't go, Mandy," Dave said.

"I'm glad you're not being rude," Jean snapped, forgetting that he had saved her life a few hours earlier. "I'd hate to see you if you were."

"Listen," Dave said, "I'm sorry, but I didn't know anything about this until this morning."

"But you have one cancellation," Jean said, wishing Johnny was present to argue their case for them. But he was busy in the hold, getting the engines ready for the cruise. Jean had no idea where Michele was, probably in the bathroom critically adjusting the shade of her lipstick. She had gotten up that morning at six as spunky as someone who had gone to bed at nine. She had immediately flipped on the TV and ordered room service. Jean loathed people who didn't need lots of sleep. "Johnny had already invited me," she continued. "So Mandy should be able to take the person who canceled's place."

"He invited you without asking me," Dave said.

"We can pay," Jean said defiantly.

Dave looked exasperated. "Money's not the issue."

"Money's always the issue," Jean said. She opened her purse. "If we pay, maybe you'll be in a better mood."

Dave put out his hand, closing her purse. "Stop that, all right? You can come. Both of you. Just don't bitch if there's no place on deck for you to sunbathe."

"Thank you," Mandy and Jean said together.

They set sail not long afterward, if *sail* could be used for a motorboat. The morning was truly glorious. Most of the west coast of Maui became visible as they moved out to sea. The small island of Molokai, where a leper colony had been, was to the north. The bow of the ship was pointed at Lanai. The sun shone on the glassy water with painful brilliance. There were few clouds in the sky, and those that were visible lay scattered to the south, hugging the green mountains of west Maui.

Jean rubbed suntan lotion on her face and pulled her sunglasses back down. Michele and Mandy sat on the rear rails beside her. The boat *was* jammed.

"This is the life," Jean said and sighed.

"Wait till the humpbacks start flying," Michele said. "Then you'll know you're in the greatest spot on earth."

They saw their first whale not long after. It burst above the surface only a hundred yards off to their right, which wasn't far considering it weighed forty tons. Everybody on the boat jumped up and applauded as the creature crashed back beneath the surface. Jean caught the spray of its departure on her face.

"You're right," she told Michele. "This is the greatest."

Jean first saw Johnny when he came up to pass out danish and coffee. She was impressed with the natural way in which he socialized with the dozen or so people aboard. He answered all their questions patiently, and with authority. He knew his islands. She was surprised to learn how young Maui was—geologically speaking—compared to Oahu, for example. Honolulu was located on Oahu. She hadn't known that the absence of lots of sandy beaches on Maui was because the coral had not had time to erode into fine sand particles yet.

Johnny finally got to their section of the boat. "Coffee, ladies?" he asked. "A doughnut? A Danish?"

"Yes, please, all three," Mandy said. She hadn't asked Jean how things had gone the previous night. Jean had remained quiet; she wasn't one to rub salt in open wounds. Mandy took the plate of dough-nuts and danish and the whole pot of coffee that Johnny was carrying. She wasn't in the mood for diets that morning.

"Didn't we have breakfast this morning?" Johnny asked Mandy.

"We didn't have much," Jean said, picking up a doughnut. "Your partner ate most of what Michele ordered."

"He told me he hassled you girls about coming," Johnny said. "I'm sorry. I told him not to."

"It was nothing," Jean said.

"Are we going to get to go diving again?" Mandy asked.

"You bet," Johnny said. "We have extra tanks. You may get to go on a couple of dives."

Jean pointed to the other people on the boat. "Are these people going on an introductory dive without any practice in the pool?"

"Yeah," Johnny said. "We'll give them a quick course out here. They'll be fine. What you did yesterday—going in the water off the beach—is far harder than what we'll do today. Here you won't have to go through waves. You'll just put the equipment on your back and step into the water. We're in luck today. The visibility is a hundred and twenty feet. That's as good as it gets. Hey, would any of you like a tour of the ship?"

"I would," Jean said. She turned to Mandy. Michele had already put her head down to sun-bathe. "How about you?"

"Michele and I were out on this boat the other day," Mandy said. "Remember, I told you."

Yeah, when you told me to leave your guy alone. Is this a hint, old friend? I'm sorry.

"I remember" was all Jean said.

The *Windspeed* was not that big, and the tour didn't last long. They visited the galley, the control area, the head, and ended up once more at the stern. There the guys had two wave runners stowed. Jean had never been on one before.

"It's like riding a motorcycle over the water," Johnny explained. "Each one carries two people. They're faster than jet skis. They can do better than thirty miles an hour if the water is glassy, like it is this morning. I can take you out after we go for a dive, if you'd like. We'll just have to be careful when we head away from the boat. We don't want to hit any diver who's resurfacing."

"What would happen if you did?" she asked.

"At full speed, we'd kill him."

Lanai rose in front of them. Every now and then a humpback would break the surface. Johnny explained to the passengers that they would not actually go onto the island. He said there wasn't much there, except pineapple plantations. But he talked in glowing terms of the spot they would throw their anchor down. He said it wasn't well known, but a whole family of sea turtles hung out there. Jean was getting excited. She had never seen a sea turtle up close.

Finally, a little less than an hour after boarding the boat, they reached their destination, a cove on the northeast side of the island. Dave shut down the engines about four hundred yards offshore. The guys handed out masks and snorkels to those who were just going snorkeling. Three passengers put on diving gear and jumped overboard, without any assistance from the guys. Johnny explained that they were already certified. The rest gathered around Dave. He covered the same skills he had the previous day. He did it quicker, however, and he used the area around the boat in place of the pool for people to practice their skills. All three of the girls went through the course again. By the time they were ready to strap on their equipment, Jean felt like an old pro.

"Would you like a partial wet suit?" Dave asked her as she picked out her snorkel and mask. She had already been in the water and found it delightfully warm.

"I don't think I need one," Jean answered.

"A suit does more than keep you warm," Dave warned. "It protects you from scratching yourself on the coral."

She glanced at the bandaged cut on her right hand. "I like the feel of the water on my skin. But I wouldn't mind a pair of gloves, if you have an extra pair."

"I'll see what I can dig up." He turned to go downstairs. She noticed the threads on the shoulder of his red wet suit where it was pulling apart. She touched them.

"You need someone to sew this up for you," she said.

He nodded. "Or I need to lose some weight."

"You're not overweight," she said.

"I know."

Finally they were all suited up. Dave had found a

bulky pair of gloves for Jean. Johnny was already in the water. Dave was helping each person off the boat. They entered using what was called the "big step method," which was an apt name. They each took a big step off the side of the boat with their fins on, holding their masks and regulators in place.

"I've put more weight on your belt," Dave said. "But the BC will keep you buoyant." He squeezed air into her vest. "I want to make sure you don't step in and sink straight to the bottom."

"You always have to look after me," she said.

"Ain't that the truth? I don't know what you do in L.A."

Jean put her regulator in her mouth and stepped off the boat. She sank briefly, but then bobbled to the surface, laughing. Mandy and Michele were already in the water.

"I want to live here!" Jean cried.

"Let's not go home," Michele agreed.

Johnny carefully let the proper amount of air out of their BCs. Their descent was totally different from the previous day. They had to slowly go down the length of the anchor rope. Jean far preferred the method to struggling through the waves. That day, however, she had trouble clearing her ears. Several times she had to go back up a few feet and blow lightly with her nostrils pinched. It was an inconvenience, nothing more. Five minutes after stepping off the boat, she was on the bottom with her friends and several other passengers.

Johnny had been right. The previous day had hardly prepared her for the stunning beauty of the coral and the breathtaking clarity of the water. Jean

checked her depth gauge. They were thirty-five feet
under, and it was as bright as midday. Fish, colored
like special-effects creatures in a sci-fi movie, swam
around them. There was no surge. They floated
weightless in the watery world. Jean couldn't remember ever having felt such serenity.

Johnny and Dave gestured for them to follow.
That day the guys had to give the new people most
of their attention. They let the three of them, even
Mandy, swim free—as long as they didn't wander
too far off. Jean paid special attention to keeping
her legs locked and her arms by her sides. She
discovered she'd automatically go in whatever direction she pointed her head.

The guys steadily led them away from the boat.
There was no seaweed in Hawaii, but there were
smaller plants of all colors and descriptions growing out of the coral. Johnny handed her a Baggie
filled with frozen peas. She clapped her hands
together, and the fish swam over. They began to eat
right out of her hand!

When they reached the family of sea turtles, Jean
was in heaven. The turtles actually seemed happy
to see them. Several of them swam over. Dave
gestured that one could rub the moss off the turtles'
shells, and they'd sit still. Jean floated up to one big
old guy and began to rub his shell, and he just
stared at her with wide black eyes. He seemed to be
saying, "Thanks, I'd rub your back if I could." Jean
wanted to lean over and kiss him.

But all too soon it was time to go up. Once more
Mandy's tank ran down to five hundred pounds per
square inch, and Dave signaled for them to return

slowly to the surface. Jean still had over a thousand psi left and felt slightly cheated. She was already hoping she could talk Johnny into letting them go on another dive. In fact, those were the first words out of her mouth when she broke the surface.

"I want to do it again," she said.

He laughed. They were about two hundred feet oceanside of the boat. "You swim in and rest and eat something," he said. "Then we'll talk about it."

They swam to the *Windspeed* facedown, using their snorkels instead of their regulators. Dave climbed aboard the boat first to help the other divers up. She was thankful for his strong arm. The instant she was out of the water, she felt the crushing weight of the equipment. Dave eased the tank off her back while she removed the weight belt.

"There's plenty of food downstairs," he said. "Help yourself."

"Thanks," she said.

The next hour passed idly. They made sandwiches out of cold cuts and drank Pepsis. Michele stretched out on the forward deck of the boat in her teeny bikini and caught the eye of all the males aboard. Mandy also sunbathed and read a romance novel. Jean followed Johnny around as he worked, pestering him about how she wanted to go back down.

He smiled. "You really fell in love with those turtles, didn't you?"

"I did," she admitted. "But I was wondering if we could take one of the wave runners and go around the other side of the island." She pointed to the spot where she meant. "When we were coming into the cove, I thought it looked like an interesting place to dive."

He had been putting regulators back into their bags when she made her remark. He suddenly stopped and stared at her intently. "Why do you say that?" he asked.

"I don't know. I just felt like I wanted to dive there."

Like I needed to dive there.

That was closer to the truth. In fact, just before they had entered the cove, she had thought the shoreline was familiar. Of course, it was possible she had seen a picture of it in her guidebook. Although, offhand, she didn't remember such a photo.

Maybe I dreamed about it.

No, that couldn't be. Her nightmare the previous night had taken place entirely underwater. The only other one she remembered recently had taken place in her hotel room. Besides, they were just dreams. They didn't mean anything.

Yeah, right. So what if they knock over catsup bottles and send me walking within inches of my death?

Jean scolded herself for thinking such thoughts. They were unproductive. They made her think she was losing her mind, or worse, that Mike hadn't really left her side.

"We'd have to go over there on a wave runner with our equipment on," Johnny said. "Then we'd have to park the runner by the shore and wade back out into the water."

"Would that be hard?" she asked.

"It would be easier to go down where we are, if all you want is another dive."

"But that's not what I want," she snapped.

He peered at her again, puzzled. "Jean?"

She blushed, embarrassed. "What I mean is, I'd really like to dive in a place I haven't been before."

"The water gets deep quick off that shore," he warned. "You'll have to be careful."

"I'll be careful."

"What's so important about that spot?" he asked.

"I don't know." She paused. She knew she was acting weird. "Do you?"

Johnny returned to stuffing his regulators back in their carrying bags. "There's some nice coral there," he muttered. "I'll take you in a few minutes."

Before the few minutes were up, Mandy heard about the plan and wanted to go, too. Johnny voiced no objection, although Jean felt uncomfortable with the idea. Again, she wasn't sure why. She wasn't worried about missing an opportunity to be alone with Johnny. She believed there would be plenty of time for that. Examining her concern, she realized she was half expecting the spot to be dangerous.

Then why do I need to dive there?

No answer. Yet the compulsion remained.

They put on their gear. Dave didn't seem to mind. His only instruction was to be back in an hour. It was getting close to noon. Dave helped Johnny get the wave runners in the water. They had to take both of them for three people. Mandy had used one before on the Colorado River and swore she knew how to handle it. She would ride on one, and Jean would hang on to Johnny's back on the other.

Johnny checked the surrounding water twice before they started out. Finally he was satisfied there were no people beneath the surface. They set out together, and Jean let out an excited cry. The thing *was* as quick as a motorcycle, and Johnny was not sparing the gas. Mandy had to try hard to keep up with them.

"How fast does this thing go?" Jean shouted, clutching him. The seat of the wave runner jumped up and down below her butt. Even with the glassy surface, it was still a bouncy ride.

"Over thirty miles an hour!" he shouted back. "On a full tank of gas it can run for over an hour and a half at full speed. You could take this from Maui to Lanai and back again if you were crazy enough."

"Why would that be crazy?" she asked.

"What if the motor quit on you in the middle of the ocean? What if waves came up?"

"Have you ever done it?" she asked.

"Once!" he shouted back.

It took them only a few minutes to go around the bend in the shore. Johnny cut his speed and Mandy caught up to them. They coasted up to the sand and climbed off the runners. The rocky ground that rose away from them was covered with wild grass and low bushes, no trees. The weight of the tanks on their backs had both girls panting.

"Let's get in the water," Jean said.

"Fine," Johnny said. "But remember to stay close to me."

Even there the water was flat. They waded away from the shore, and Johnny allowed Jean to adjust the air in her own BC. It was easy—there was a button that inflated it and another button that deflated it. The key was balance, to reach the exact right amount of air to keep one from sinking too swiftly, but still not causing one to bob to the surface. Jean remembered Dave's name for it— neutral buoyancy.

They began their descent. The coral was not so spectacular as at the other spot. It was not so colorful, and there were fewer fish. Still, the coral protruded from the floor of the ocean far higher, the shadows of it stretching across the few visible plants. Jean had the impression they were entering an older part of the island. She wondered if that was possible, if the island had been formed in stages, rather than all at once. She made a mental note to ask Johnny later.

One thing for sure—he had been right about the bottom falling away quickly. They were only a hundred and fifty feet from the shore when the coral fell off into dark blue water. Johnny gestured for them to steer away from the cliff. Jean glanced at her depth gauge. They were already in thirty feet of water. She turned to obey Johnny's instruction. Mandy did likewise. But Mandy was close to Johnny and turned too quickly. She bumped his elbow.

Her regulator popped out of her mouth.

Mandy must have been in the act of inhaling when the accident occurred. Jean saw her face contort. She was choking. She didn't even reach to find her regulator. She immediately tried to dash for the surface, a normal panicky reaction. Johnny was at her side in a second. He grabbed her and pulled her back down before she had ascended three feet. He found her regulator and held it in front of her mask so she could see it. Mandy shook her head desperately, trying to fight him off. Johnny's grip on her arm remained firm. He shook her roughly and pressed her regulator right into her face mask. He was trying to tell her that she had air with her, that she had to deal with the situation where she was.

Jean's heart pounded as she watched. She remembered all too well the danger of an air embolism. If Mandy rushed to the surface while she was choking, with her mouth closed, the air in her lungs would have no place to expand. The pressure would build, her lungs would rupture, and she might die.

Johnny finally did get through to Mandy. She took the regulator in her mouth, and Johnny used the purge valve on the back of it to blow out the water in the mouthpiece. He might have blown some of the water *into* her mouth—he didn't make Mandy stop and block her mouth with the back of her tongue—but he probably figured the priority was to get her breathing off her regulator again. Jean watched anxiously as Mandy hungrily gulped air from the hose. Johnny handled her masterfully, keeping his hand firmly on her arm and nodding his head in encouragement. Within a couple of minutes Mandy's signs of panic vanished. Johnny made a thumbs-up gesture to her. Did she want to go to the surface? She nodded her head. Johnny turned to Jean, making another thumbs-up sign. There was no arguing with him. They had to go up. The dive was less than ten minutes old.

Jean had no intention of disobeying Johnny. But as they started up, her weight belt began to loosen. It wasn't about to fall off, but she thought she should pause in her ascent to tighten it. As she did so, she noticed that Johnny was still holding on to Mandy and was paying no attention to her. Slowly the other two floated above her head.

Then Jean made a mistake of her own. As she opened the clasp on the weight belt, it slipped out of her fingers. It wasn't a panic situation like Mandy's breathing in water. The weight belt did slide off her left hip, but she was able to grab it with her other hand and keep it from sliding down to the bottom. Actually, she was only a few feet from the coral floor, which was at the edge of the cliff Johnny had gestured them away from. As she thought about it, she decided it would be easier to go back to the bottom, kneel down, and put the weight belt on there. That way she wouldn't be spinning a dozen different ways in midwater.

Careful not to let the weight belt slip away—she knew if it did she would zoom for the surface—she turned her head down and used the kick Dave had taught her to drive her toward the coral. There she grabbed a pointed rock with her free hand and secured herself by tucking her fins under an out-stretched rock. Now even if she did lose her weight belt, she thought, she would still be able to stay on the bottom. Johnny would just have to come back down to get her. She complimented herself on how cool and collected she was acting.

She didn't lose her weight belt. Now that she was safe on the bottom, and could use both her hands, she would have had to have been a klutz to do that. She wrapped it back around her waist and tight-ened it carefully. A glance up showed her that Johnny and Mandy had already reached the sur-face. The proper thing to do would be to kick up easily using her fins and rejoin them.

But Jean didn't want to do that just yet. For one thing she was enjoying sitting on the bottom by herself. It was very peaceful. Also, Mandy had—one way or another—cut short each dive Jean had taken so far. Dave said Mandy was simply an air hog and couldn't help it. But Jean didn't want Mandy to wreck this dive completely. It might be her last one for a long time. Jean thought if she stayed on the bottom, and Mandy recovered suffi-ciently on the surface, Johnny might be more inclined to allow Mandy to come back down and continue the dive.

If I go back up right now, he will definitely call it a day.

So the idea of having more fun kept Jean down. Her next idea came out of nowhere, and it carried with it the force of something totally alien. Jean bobbed over to the edge of the cliff and glanced down. The water was so clear. She figured even if she went all the way to the bottom, she'd be able to see.

A strange feeling swept over her.

It was as if an invisible net had been dropped over her from above or below and was pulling on her.

Something down there was calling to her.

Jean glanced back up at the surface. Johnny was still preoccupied with Mandy. Jean tried to remember everything he had said earlier about diving deeper than forty feet. It hadn't sounded difficult.

"It's no harder to go down to a hundred feet than forty feet, Jean. You just have to keep clearing your ears and not hurry yourself. But once you're down there, a few things are different. One, you have to put more air in your BC to maintain neutral buoyancy. Also, your air is used up much more rapidly, two or three times as fast. That's because it's under more pressure. You can't stay down long—eighteen minutes max if you want to have a nondecompression dive. Fifteen minutes would be a long time. But it's when you come back up that you have to be extra cautious. You must come up very slowly, and when you reach a depth of fifteen feet, you have to stop for three minutes. If you don't, you risk getting the bends. Diving beyond a hundred feet you risk getting narced—that's where the nitrogen is forced into your blood, and you act like you're drunk. Never dive deeper than a hundred feet until you're real experienced."

He had later explained that a nondecompression dive meant a dive that did not require an elaborate series of stops on the ascent. She had asked what was the deepest dive he'd ever attempted. A hundred and eighty feet, he had replied. She was impressed.

I could just go down there for a few minutes.

But why risk it? What was the source of this compulsion? Her nightmares? She didn't see any bloody bath down there. She couldn't even see a cave.

Jean glanced up once more. If she was going to do it, she was going to have to do it in the next few seconds. She could tell Johnny that she accidentally let too much air out of her BC and sank. He'd understand. Besides, then she could brag to the other girls about how deep she had gone.

She pulled herself closer to the edge of the watery cliff. Why she decided to go was not logical. She did it merely because she wanted to.

Jean pushed herself off the cliff, floating effortlessly in the blue void, the floor of the ocean at least another sixty feet below her dangling fins. She raised the black hose of her BC and let a little air escape. Almost immediately she began to sink, but she was careful to buffet her descent with a slight kicking motion of her fins. The coral wall in front of her drifted slowly upward. The number of fish thinned dramatically. She kept her nostrils pinched the whole way down, clearing continuously. The deeper she went, the louder the popping sound her ears made. She wasn't afraid. She felt in total control of the situation. The glassy surface receded until it looked as if it were a mile above her.

Finally she reached the bottom, or the first

bottom; the cliff took deeper plunges only a few yards away. But she had gone as deep as she planned. The sunlight had dimmed considerably. The water appeared a much deeper blue. She checked her gauge.

Oh, God.

There were a hundred and three feet of water above her.

Now that she had reached the bottom, she thought maybe it was time to start back up. Her compulsion had lessened. She assumed it was one of those things people felt they had to do, and then once they did it, it didn't matter to them anymore. She tapped a little air into her BC and regained neutral buoyancy. She would swim up slow as a snail and blame her radical descent on her equipment.

Then she saw the cave. It was off to her left, about a hundred feet away. It cut into the cliff wall at a sharp angle. Jean suspected that the walls of the cave were not solid, that light filtered in from the sides and even the ceiling. She swam toward it. She told herself she just wanted to have a look, and then she'd return to Johnny and Mandy on the surface.

The opening was as tall as a man, and she hovered in front of it, wondering where it led. The pull it exerted on her was tremendous. She envisioned swimming into it and finding a secret cavern glowing with gems. But that was only part of it. The cave was very familiar.

It's the one from my dream.

It was true. It was Mike's cave. If she swam inside, she thought, she'd find no treasure, but she would have to travel once more through her memory of his death. Light glittered in the depths of the cave—sunlight, not the cold rays of the moon. It didn't matter. The mystery of the cave remained. Her dreams had to have been more than dreams to have so accurately shown her a place she had never visited.

Jean had to make another decision, or maybe there really was no decision at all, maybe she only acted out a predestined and inevitable response. She swam forward into the cave. She would just have a peek, she told herself, and then return to the surface.

The way opened before her. Her earlier guess had been correct. The cave ran along the cliff wall—its own walls were not entirely solid. She had some light to see by. The bubbles from her regulator gathered around cracks in the ceiling and then vanished, as if sucked away by a hungry animal concealed in the coral. Forty feet into the cave it split in three directions. The main path led straight forward. Another curved upward. The final way was more of a tunnel. It turned to the right, deeper into the side of the cliff. Jean could see at a glance that she would need a flashlight to go in there, even if she could fit. Of course, there was no possibility she would go in there. Or so she thought.

In the dream Mike led me into a tunnel off the main cave.

Jean floated toward the narrow opening. She supposed she could go in a little bit. There would be enough light for maybe thirty feet. That was only ten yards—a mere first down in football. The worst that could happen to her, if it got too narrow, is that she would have to back out. That should be simple; she could use the sides of the tunnels as handholds.

Why are you doing this? You have to get back to the surface!

Jean checked her watch. She had been on the bottom less than ten minutes. She was well within a sensible safety margin, if the information Johnny had given her was correct. She could spare a couple of more minutes.

Jean swam into the tunnel. Head first.

She was about fifteen feet in when she decided there was no way she was going to make it to thirty feet. Already it was so dark she could hardly see. She decided to go back. She had seen enough, anyway, which was really nothing at all. The stone walls of the tunnel were featureless. She figured if she could just squeeze out a hundred and eighty degree turn, it would be easier than trying to retrace her steps butt first. There appeared to be enough room.

Jean started to turn around.

Then she heard a clang of metal on stone and her turn came to an abrupt halt. She shoved with the back of her tank. It slid a couple of inches more and then stopped again. It wouldn't budge an inch. She was balled up in the tunnel like a fetus. She decided to slide the tank back to its original position. She would back out of the cave, after all.

But the tank couldn't move. It was stuck. She was stuck.

Don't panic.

She began to panic.

Jean consumed a great deal of air in those next few minutes. She consumed the one thing she could not spare. She tried in vain to calm herself as she kept checking her watch. The second hand seemed to have gained fresh speed. It swung around the dial once, twice, three times. She realized she had been at a depth of slightly over a hundred feet for fifteen minutes. She had three minutes to get free if she didn't want to suffer the bends and perhaps six minutes to get loose before she would drown. She threw herself with all her strength to the right, to the left.

She remained locked in place.

Oh, God, help me.

In all the nightmares she had ever had, throughout her entire life, nothing had been as bad as this. But the fun was not over. She twisted her head from side to side, looking for Johnny, praying he had had enough sense to follow her into the cave.

It was then she saw the skull.

It floated in the depths of the tunnel, a ball of sickly white in a void of black. A splintered hole the size of a silver dollar could be seen on the right side near the temple. It gaped at her like a mutated third eye.

Jean screamed. In silence.

Her regulator popped out of her mouth.

The skull saved her life. It scared her so much that it made her shove away from it with such force that she broke free of her jam. Metal scraped against stone and then stopped. She whirled, turning her back to the skull and her head toward the tunnel exit. She thrashed several powerful strokes with her fins, with her breath held. In fact she was out of the tunnel, back in the main cave, before she even reached for her regulator. Quickly she put it in her mouth, blocked off her windpipe with the back of her tongue, and used the purge valve. Salt water squirted around her teeth and then was gone. She drank in the air as hungrily as Mandy had after choking.

I've got to get out of here!

Jean checked her air gauge. She had two hundred psi left in her tank. Pressing her arms against her sides, trying to breathe conservatively, she swam toward the entrance of the cave. She ended up breathing about as easily as someone who had just seen a ghost, which she felt was not far from the truth.

She swam for a long time, much longer than she could remember having done on the way in.

Then she ran into a dead end.

Someone had walled up the entrance to the cave!

But that was impossible. She realized in an instant what she had done. Exiting the tunnel, she had turned to the right instead of the left. This whole time she had been swimming *deeper* into the cave. She checked her air gauge again. She was down to one hundred and forty psi. She quickly turned over and shoved off the coral wall. It was probably already too late for her.

Two minutes later Jean burst out of the cave at high speed.

It was then something grabbed her leg from behind.

No!

Jean kicked with both her legs, not looking at what had ahold of her. It was enough to get her free. She turned her head toward the surface, feeling as if she had a monster on her tail, and began to claw upward with her arms, abandoning every rule she had learned. She didn't have to look at her gauge. She knew it had already lost another hundred psi. She was willing to suffer the bends before she was going to drown or be eaten.

She had ascended maybe twenty feet when she felt her right leg grabbed again. This time she was unable to shake loose. She began to cry inside her mask. She was being pulled back down! She was going to die! Mike was going to have her for dinner!

It was not Mike, though, but Johnny. He pulled her down to his level and shook his head vigorously. He grabbed her depth and air gauges and kept shaking her head. He reached into the side of his BC vest and drew out a long yellow hose with a spare regulator at the end of it. He pressed it into her face mask and nodded his head. Jean just stared at it. She didn't know what it was. She didn't know what he wanted her to do with it. She was in shock. But she was glad to see Johnny had flesh behind his face mask and not bone. His eyes seemed to speak to her.

It's called an octopus, Jean. Don't you remember? We told you about it before your first ocean dive. You can breathe off it; it's a spare regulator. It lets you use my air. Just put it in your mouth, purge the water, and you won't die.

Jean put the octopus in her mouth, got rid of the water, and began to breathe. Johnny put his coupled hands to his head as if he were taking a nap. He was trying to tell her to relax. He took firm hold of her free arm and made her take hold of his other arm. They started toward the surface. Slowly.

They went up to forty-five feet. There Johnny made them stop. Jean didn't understand. Weren't they allowed to go all the way to fifteen feet? She would have felt a lot more comfortable there. Then she realized Johnny was treating her dive as a nondecompression dive—one to be handled more carefully. She understood that if he hadn't gotten to her when he did, and she had just gone straight up like a balloon, she probably would have died.

Johnny checked his air gauge. He had only two hundred psi, and it was going down fast because they were both breathing off his tank. Yet he kept them at a depth of forty-five feet for three minutes, before he let them ascend to fifteen feet. Once there Jean had to resist the temptation to bolt for the surface. Johnny's air gauge was now at fifty psi. Yet he was patient. He let it sink close to zero before gesturing that she was to start breathing off her own regulator. She made the switch without difficulty. Johnny checked his watch. She realized he had far less air left than she did. She just hoped his experience would let him drag it out. He held her gauge in hand the whole time he waited. She knew they were both going to come up with zero air left.

And that was what happened. When her gauge hit zero, she suddenly had trouble drawing in air through her regulator. Johnny cautioned her one last time not to panic and then slowly led her up to the surface. Once there she spit out her regulator and gasped at the fresh air. Johnny reached over and grabbed her BC valve. Because she didn't have any air left in her tank, he had to inflate it manually, blowing with his mouth. In seconds she was floating comfortably on the surface.

"Now I want you to relax and breathe easily," he said. "We can talk when we get in."

"Oh, God," she whispered, letting the oxygen flush into her system, loving the warmth of the sun on her face.

"That's it, Jean. Just lie back and close your eyes and breathe." He turned her around so that her back was to him. "I am going to grab the valve at the top of your tank and tow you in. Don't do anything. Don't kick your fins, don't use your arms. Leave everything to me."

"OK," she said softly.

He towed her into the shallow water as if she were a sleeping walrus. When he was able to stand, he removed his fins and deflated her BC. He made her take off her fins and held her as he helped her onto the sand, where Mandy waited expectantly.

"Are you OK?" Mandy cried. "What happened?"

"I'm fine," Jean said. She let Johnny unhook the equipment off her back, and then she collapsed to the ground. She sat for a minute, every muscle in her body shuddering with exhaustion. Johnny and Mandy stood silently over her. She closed her eyes and felt tears trickle over her cheeks. "I'm fine," she finally said again.

"What happened?" Mandy asked.

Jean opened her eyes. She wiped off her face. "I don't know."

Johnny shook his head and stepped away. "Right," he muttered.

"I accidentally sank down," Jean said.

Johnny whirled around, his face angry. "You went down on purpose! You did it because you thought it would be fun! Well, was it fun? You came within two breaths of dying, do you know that? If I hadn't caught you when you came out of that cave, you'd be rolling around on the ground right now with nitrogen bubbles in your blood big enough to wreck you permanently."

"I'm sorry," she said weakly.

"You're sorry?" He was disgusted. "I'm sorry I ever invited you on this trip. You're a foolish girl, Jean. You should stay away from the water."

"I said I'm sorry. What else can I say?"

"You could say thank you for saving your life," he said.

She bowed her head. "I am thankful."

"What were you doing in that cave anyway?" he asked.

"What cave?" Mandy asked.

"There's a cave at a depth of about a hundred feet," Johnny explained. "No one with any brains goes in it. What were you doing in there, Jean?"

She met his gaze directly. She may have been ashamed at the trouble she had caused him, but she wasn't a three-year-old. She hated to be scolded.

"I was looking at a human skull I'd found," she said.

He snorted. "Get off it."

Mandy smiled. "You're kidding, aren't you?"

Jean stood up slowly, her legs unsteady, her voice firm. "I saw what I saw. It's in a narrow tunnel off the main cave. You go in about forty or fifty feet and the tunnel's on your right. The skull is about twenty-five feet inside. It's just floating there in the middle."

"You were hallucinating," Johnny said.

"No way," Jean said. "It's there."

Johnny sighed. "You are inexperienced. You were down over a hundred feet. You got narced. You saw something that wasn't there. The same thing has happened to me when I've dived too deep. Once I thought I saw a mermaid. It was a plant. There is no skull in the tunnel."

"I was not hallucinating," Jean insisted.

"Jean," Mandy said. "Why don't you believe Johnny?"

"Because it's there!"

Johnny put his hands on his hips and yawned. "I'm getting tired of this. We have to get back to the boat."

Jean took a step forward. "Why don't you go back down there and check it out?"

"With what?" Johnny asked.

Jean pointed to Mandy's tank. "Mandy was down only a few minutes. Use her air. That is, if you have the guts."

Johnny acted bored. "Actually, I don't have the guts. I was just down past a hundred feet. If I go

127

back down right now, I'll get the bends. I have to wait several hours before I can dive to any kind of depth."

"Then what about Dave?" Jean asked.

"What about him?" Johnny asked.

"I want him to look for the skull."

Johnny chuckled. "The chance of him doing that is pretty remote."

"Ask him," Jean insisted.

Johnny shook his head. "This is crazy."

"He might do it, you know. Where did the *Moonflower* sink?"

"It was right around here." He paused. "How did you know that?"

How did I know what an underwater cave looked like before I saw it?

"I didn't," she said. "I just guessed."

Johnny knew she was implying that the skull might belong to Ringo. He stared at her a moment, then finally nodded his head. He slipped out of his equipment and walked toward one of the wave runners. "You two stay here and rest. I'm going back to the boat. I'll tell Dave what you saw, Jean."

"Good," she said.

Dave returned with Johnny ten minutes later, riding on the back of the wave runner in full diving gear. Jean was happy to see him until he climbed onto the beach and started yelling at her.

"What's this I hear about you diving down to a hundred feet?" Dave demanded.

"I've already chewed her out about it," Johnny said.

"And I've already said I'm sorry a half dozen times," Jean said.

Dave studied her. "How are you feeling?"

She shrugged. "I'm still a little shook up. I'm exhausted."

"Do you have any pain in your joints?" Dave asked.

"No. I don't have the bends."

Dave shook a finger at her. "You might have them and not know it yet. We have to keep an eye on you for the next few hours. If you're bent, we're going to have to get you to a decompression chamber."

That sobered Jean somewhat. "I won't do it again."

"All right," Dave growled. He glanced at Mandy, who was resting on a towel on the ground. "And how are you? I heard you took in a lungful of salt water?"

"I'm fine," Mandy said.

"Good," Dave said. "That happens to the best of us sometimes." He turned back to Jean. "Tell me what you saw."

He listened patiently while she related her story, more patiently than Johnny had. But when she was done, he remained unconvinced.

"You were jammed in a tight place over a hundred feet down," Dave said. "Your air was running low. It was probably a hallucination."

"I don't hallucinate," she said briskly. "Why don't you give me the benefit of the doubt and look?"

Dave turned to Johnny. "It's been over two hours

since our first dive," Dave said. "We didn't go below thirty-five feet. What do you think?"

"You should be OK," Johnny said. "Do you have a flashlight?"

"Yeah."

"Don't get stuck in the tunnel like Jean did," Johnny warned. "Don't stay down too long."

"I'll be back in twenty minutes," Dave said. He put on his mask and walked into the water. He was a powerful swimmer. He slipped on his fins and waded out to the spot where Jean estimated the cliff began. He disappeared in a sudden splash. Johnny was ill at ease.

"Cave diving is never a smart idea when you're alone," he said. "You should always have a buddy with you."

Jean felt guilty. "We could have come back tomorrow and looked."

"We have to go to another part of the island tomorrow," he said.

"You're really mad at me, aren't you?"

Johnny took a breath and let it out. "No, it's me I'm mad at. Mandy was having a hard time catching her breath even on the surface. I took my eyes off you for too long. An experienced instructor should never do that." He looked at her and a portion of his old grin returned. "I'm sorry for blowing up at you. You just scared me. When I went down and couldn't find you, I thought you might be dead."

"How did you happen to be waiting outside the cave?" she asked.

"I saw your bubbles eventually," he said. He was puzzled. "Why did you go in there, of all places?"

Jean stared out over the water. She could see Dave's bubbles. "I had a dream about that cave," she whispered.

"What?" Johnny asked.

"Was that the cave in your dream?" Mandy asked in disbelief. Jean had told her that morning about her nightmares. Jean had immediately regretted it. Mandy had given her the strangest look, kind of similar to the one she was giving her now.

"No," Jean said.

"What's all this about?" Johnny asked.

"Nothing," she said. "Let's see what Dave finds."

Dave returned twenty minutes later, as promised. He shook his head as he pulled off his mask. "There's no skull in that cave," he said.

"But it's there!" Jean protested.

"It's not there," Dave insisted. "You got narced. You just thought you saw it."

"But are you sure you had the right tunnel?" she asked. "You must have been looking in the wrong place. I didn't imagine it."

"I was in the same tunnel as you," Dave said. "I could see where your tank had scraped the coral when you got stuck. There was no skull in that place, and I went in a lot farther than you did." He glanced at his watch. "Now it's almost two o'clock. We're going to drop this. We have to get our people back to Maui. We'll be an hour late as it is. Johnny, you take Jean on your wave runner. I'll take Mandy on mine. Let's go." He looked at Jean and Mandy. "Don't either of you mention this skull thing to anybody on board."

"I won't say anything," Mandy said.

"But—" Jean protested.

"Later," Johnny said. "Just do as Dave says. Please?"

"All right," Jean said, trying not to sulk.

They arrived back at the *Windspeed* in a few minutes. Dave wasted no time raising the anchor. Soon they were under way. Lanai fell behind them. Jean sat up front with the girls. Michele rolled over in her bikini, her tan better than ever.

"I heard you almost drowned," Michele said.

"It was close," Jean muttered. She thought of the skull, and the splintered hole on the temple area. It could have been a bullet hole. The person could have been shot at close range. "It was very close," she told Michele.

CHAPTER
NINE

An hour and a half later they were safely docked, and all the passengers were off the boat. The guys walked the girls to the parking lot. Jean noticed that Johnny had brought his car. While the group was discussing what they were going to do next, Jean interrupted.

"Could Johnny and I go somewhere by ourselves?" she asked.

Michele laughed. "Where do you want to go, back to the hotel?"

"God, Jean," Mandy said, hurt. "Don't you think you're being rude?"

"I'm sorry," Jean said. She didn't really mean it. At the moment she was too concerned about losing her mind. She turned to Johnny. "Would that be OK?"

He shrugged. "It's fine with me. Can you guys get Dave home or wherever he wants to go in your rental?" They said it would be fine, although Mandy continued to act annoyed. "Where are we going?" Johnny asked Jean.

"I don't know," she said honestly.

The group split in two. Since she didn't give him any instructions, Johnny drove in the direction of the hotel. The time was a quarter to four. Jean fretted in her seat.

"Something weird is going on here," she said finally.

"What is it?" Johnny asked.

"You still don't believe I saw the skull, do you?"

He spoke carefully. "Frankly, no. But that doesn't mean I think you're crazy. I told you I've been narced before. It can happen to anybody."

Jean had to chuckle. "Maybe if I told you what I've been going through the last couple of days, you *would* think I was crazy."

Johnny suddenly pulled over to the side of the road. He turned off the engine and put his elbow on the back of her seat, twisting his body toward her.

"Tell me," he said.

What could she do? He could see already that she was acting off-balance. If she gave him the background, he might have more patience with her. She began with Mike dying on the plane beside her, and then went on to describe both nightmares. She finished with a detailed account of the hole in the side of the skull. Johnny listened without making a sound. When she was done, he still sat thoughtfully and silently.

"What do you think?" she had to ask.

He swallowed. "Those are strange stories. Your

dream was the reason you dived to the bottom today?"

"Yes."

"That was a dangerous dream to have. What did you say the boy's name was?"

"Mike Clyde. I'll never forget it." She paused. "What's the matter?"

"Nothing."

"You suddenly blinked. Do you know that name?"

He frowned. "It seems familiar somehow."

"How?"

"I don't know." He chewed on his lower lip, staring past her into the middle distance. "You say the flight attendant seemed to know this Mike?"

"Yeah. I guess she talked to him on the plane before he moved into the seat beside me. I've thought of calling the airline and getting her number and talking to her about him." She came to a decision. "In fact, why don't I do that right now? Let's drive to a phone booth."

Johnny didn't seem pleased with the idea. "Why talk to her? Mike's dead. He doesn't have anything to do with what's going on with you."

"But I explained to you about the dreams. They showed me things I shouldn't or couldn't have known."

"Jean, be sensible. Dreams are dreams. They're meaningless."

"But what about the catsup falling in the bath when I was dreaming about a blood-filled tub? What about the cave? I *saw* that cave in my dream."

"Most of the caves off Lanai look the same."

"But the skull!" she said.

"There was no skull. Dave would have seen it if it was there."

Jean tried to relax but ended up fuming. "I want to talk to the flight attendant. She was interested in Mike. They may have done an autopsy on him. I want to know what killed him."

"Jean, you say he died on the plane beside you. He didn't drown. No one shot him in the head."

"I still want to talk to her."

Johnny sighed. He restarted the car. "All right. If it'll make you happy."

They drove back to the harbor. Johnny parked his car in the same spot it had occupied all day. He didn't follow her to the phone booth because he wanted to get a shirt off the boat.

Jean found a phone in a restaurant that had a view of the late-afternoon sky over the harbor. She called information and got the number of Trans Island Airlines. But when she called the airlines, they didn't want to give out the number where Patricia was staying on the island. It was against their policy.

"But this is a personal matter," Jean complained. "It's important that I reach her immediately."

"Do you know Patricia?" the man on the other end asked.

"I only met her on the plane yesterday. But she'll remember me. Look, my name's Jean Fiscal. I'm an eighteen-year-old high school student. I'm not some crazy rapist or something."

"The best I can do is have her call you where you're staying," the man said.

"I'm in a phone booth right now."

"Give me the number there, and I'll call Patricia right now."

Jean figured it was worth a shot. She hovered near the phone while she waited, staring out the restaurant window at the harbor. She could see Johnny in the distance, climbing onto his boat. She waited only a couple of minutes before the phone rang. It was not the man at the airlines, but Patricia herself. Jean quickly asked the woman if she remembered her.

"Of course," Patricia said. "You were a friend of Mike's."

"Mike's the reason I'm calling. Have you heard anything about how he died?"

There was a long pause. "No. Just what I read in the papers."

"There was an article about him in the paper?" Jean asked.

"Yeah. The Maui *Herald* did a short piece on him."

Jean wrote down the name on a piece of paper beside the phone. "What did they say?" she asked.

Patricia groaned. "It was gruesome. The doctors say it was pressure-related. His lungs had ruptured. They think he was down too deep and came up too quick."

Jean was confused. "You mean in the plane?"

"No, in the sea. Mike died scuba diving."

"Wait. What are you talking about? We both met Mike on the plane."

Patricia was taken back. *"I* met him on the plane. I don't know where you met him."

All of a sudden Jean didn't feel good. In fact, she felt as if she was about to be sick. "But I was on the same plane, with both of you," she said. "You said you remembered me?"

"I thought I recognized your name. I might have you confused with someone else. You're Jean Fiscal, right? You were on the flight that came in yesterday morning?"

"Yeah. I was on the flight with Mike."

There was another long pause. "Are we talking about the same Mike? Mike Clyde?"

"Yeah," Jean said, getting exasperated. "He died on the plane yesterday."

"No. Mike died a month ago while scuba diving off Lanai."

Jean closed her eyes and put her hand to her head. Blood roared in her ears. "But I saw him yesterday," she said desperately.

"We must be talking about two different people. Mike came here—" Patricia suddenly stopped. "Oh, God."

"What is it?" Jean asked.

"It can't be."

"Tell me!" Jean demanded.

Patricia's voice was unsteady. "Why do you say Mike died on the plane?"

"Because I saw him die! He was sitting right beside me. We were talking, and then he began to choke and gasp for air. He fell into the aisle. Then you came running over and did CPR on him. But it didn't help. Blood spurted out of his mouth. He was dead. You know what happened. You were there. We talked about it as I was leaving the plane."

"I didn't know what you were talking about," Patricia said. "I just thought you were a friend of Mike's."

Jean was lost. "How did you meet Mike?" she asked, trying to put the pieces together.

"I met him a month ago on a flight when he was coming to Hawaii. He was all excited. He had won the trip in a magazine contest. He told me he had never even seen the ocean before. He was such a nice boy. I gave him my phone number so I could introduce him to a cousin of mine and let her show him around. He called once, but my cousin was busy that day. He said he'd call back. But then I read about him in the paper a few days later." Patricia took a breath. "But you say you met him on the plane—yesterday. That's impossible."

"I did meet him," Jean said. "I'm not crazy. He told me all about the trip he won, too. I can even tell you what town he was from—Hoker, Alabama."

Patricia gasped. "That's right."

"You were going to say something a moment ago. What was it? What can't be?"

Patricia spoke reluctantly. "After you got off the plane, I thought what a coincidence it was that you were given the seat you were in—your being a friend of Mike's and all. I wondered if you had requested it."

"What was o strange about the seat I was in?" Jean already knew the answer.

"You're sitting in my seat."

"You were sitting in the seat Mike had sat in when he came to Hawaii," Patricia said.

Jean almost fainted. "What does this mean?" she whispered.

"It sounds like you're either pulling my leg, or you were talking to a ghost."

"I'm not pulling your leg," Jean mumbled.

Patricia thought a moment. "No, it doesn't sound as if you are."

"Did anybody else on my flight see Mike die?"

"No. To tell you the truth, dear, you slept most of the entire flight."

That was true. She had only woken up to talk to Mike.

"He's been dead a whole month?" Jean had to ask again.

"I'm afraid so. I don't know what else to tell you. This is damn peculiar."

Jean felt claustrophobic, as if she were once again trapped in an underwater tunnel. "What did they do with his body?" she asked.

"I believe he was buried on the island. I'd have to check the article to be sure."

"Do you have it handy?"

"No. I'm sure I threw it out."

"I have to go now," Jean suddenly blurted out. "Could I talk to you later?"

Patricia was concerned and said yes. "Are you going to be all right, dear?"

"I'll be just fine. Thanks."

Jean hung up the phone and sagged against the wall of the booth.

It was just a dream, after all. But a dream about a dead boy I had never met. This whole trip has been nothing but a nightmare. The blood in the bathtub. The cave. The skeleton.

Whose skull had she seen? And why hadn't Dave seen it? Had she been asleep underwater? Somehow, despite everything Patricia had said, she doubted it. At least, on the plane she had started her adventure into ghostland by falling asleep. The same with the bloody bathtub. But out on the reef she had been fully alert, with all her senses working on high.

The skull was real, and Mike was trying to show it to me.

But why?

Jean left the restaurant and ran into Johnny as he was walking back to his car. "What did you find out?" he asked.

"That Mike Clyde's been dead for a month."

"But you said he was on your flight."

"I did, didn't I," she said. "Well, I was wrong. It was his astral body that was on the plane."

Johnny squinted. "What's an astral body?"

"Never mind. The flight attendant told me that Mike died scuba diving off the Lanai coast. Does that ring a bell with you?"

Johnny snapped his fingers. "I knew I'd heard that name somewhere."

"How come you just remembered his name now?" she asked suspiciously.

Johnny was offended. "You were asking me about someone you had just met. How was I supposed to connect him with someone we taught to scuba dive over a month ago."

"*You* taught him how to dive?"

"I didn't teach him personally. He went through the course at the hotel. Dave gave him his instructions. But it wasn't Dave's fault he died. I understand Mike wasn't even certified when he took a hundred-foot dive." Johnny nodded. "Sort of like you did this afternoon," he said pointedly.

"Where did Mike die?"

"You said it yourself. Off Lanai."

"Where exactly?"

Johnny shrugged. "I don't know."

"Where is the office for the Maui *Herald* located?"

"In Lahaina. Why?"

"I want to go there. I want to read about what happened to Mike."

"Why?" he asked.

"I have to figure this thing out. Do you want to take me or not? I can catch a cab if you don't want to."

Johnny peered at her strangely. "You're not having any aching in your joints, are you?"

"No."

"Are you sure?" he asked.

"I'm not suffering from the bends."

"Still, maybe you should go back to the hotel and rest."

"Why?" she snapped. "So I can have another

dream? I've had enough already, thank you. I'm going to solve this mystery."

"What's the mystery?" he asked.

"How Mike died."

Johnny showed impatience. "I can tell you how he died. He dived too deep. He came up too quick. That's the end of the story. Now, drop it, Jean. For your own good. You're driving yourself crazy."

"I can't." She touched his arm. "Look, I know I'm being weird. Why don't you go back to the hotel and team up with the others? Have some fun. I'll catch up with you later."

Johnny shook his head. "I'll take you to the *Herald*. But then you've got to promise me you'll forget about Mike Clyde."

"We'll see," Jean said.

They reached the office fifteen minutes later. Nothing was very far away on Maui. The time was twenty minutes to five. The place was about to close. Jean asked the kind-faced elderly woman at the front desk if she could look at month-old editions of the *Herald*.

"Sure," the woman said, leading the two of them to a side door. "The stacks are in the back. Do you have a particular date in mind?"

Jean glanced at Johnny, who shook his head. "No," she said. "I'll have to search through the papers."

The woman glanced at her watch. "You're going to have to be quick."

It took Jean no time at all to find what she

wanted. The article was on the front page of the March 10 edition. There was no picture. She spread it out on a desk so that Johnny could read it with her.

INEXPERIENCED DIVER DROWNS OFF LANAI

By Ralph Simpson

The body of a visitor, Mike Clyde, was found floating facedown in the water Tuesday morning on the northeast side of Lanai. Except for a missing weight belt, he was in full diving gear. Clyde was nineteen years old and was from Hoker, Alabama. He was visiting Maui because he had won a contest in a magazine.

Clyde had only recently begun a scuba course and was not yet certified. He was found alone in the water, with no boat nearby. How he reached Lanai is a mystery. The police are contacting all boat owners in the area to see if any of them took him to the island.

An autopsy performed on Clyde last night reveals the probable cause of death to be a sudden rise to the surface after a prolonged deep dive. Both of Clyde's lungs had ruptured because of major air embolisms. Samples of his brain tissue also showed he had suffered multiple strokes.

The reading on his depth gauge confirms part of this theory. He had been down to a depth of one hundred and ten feet. The absence of his weight belt is being considered in the matter. It is possible it slipped off and caused his sudden return to the surface. But so far the authorities have been unable to locate the weight belt on the floor of the ocean. An investigation is continuing.

Clyde is to be buried this Saturday at Happy Point Memorial Cemetery. The police say he has no surviving family.

"What do you think?" Jean asked. She still hadn't adjusted to the idea that Mike had been dead a month when she met him. A picture would have made it easier for her to accept.

"It's just what I said," Johnny replied. "In fact, I've already read this article."

"How come you didn't tell me?"

"Because I didn't remember, Jean. Maui's not that small that people don't die here regularly. I didn't purposely keep information from you."

"I'm sorry. I didn't mean to imply that you had. What do you think about the part about there being no boat in the area? How would you explain that?"

"Easily," Johnny said. "Somebody took him out on a dive he wasn't experienced enough to go on, and he died. Then the person or people on the boat panicked and fled the area. They were probably afraid they'd be sued."

"What about Mike's weight belt?"

"It must have fallen off. That happens."

"Yes, it does," Jean said thoughtfully. "Did you notice where he was found? On the northeast side of Lanai. That was where we were today. Does that surprise you?"

"No. Should it?"

"You said that was where the *Moonflower* went down."

"That's true," Johnny said. "But the *Moonflower* sank a year ago. Mike died a month ago. The two events aren't connected."

"Are you sure?"

"Jean, it doesn't say where Mike was found on the northeast side of Lanai. It could have been anywhere. That's a good stretch of coast there."

"Is there any way to find out exactly where it was?" she asked.

"You could ask the police. You could ask Dave. He might know."

"I don't want to ask Dave."

"Why not?" Johnny took a step back and groaned. "Don't tell me. Now Dave's under suspicion?"

"I didn't say that."

"You were about to."

"No, I wasn't," she said. "Don't even tell Dave I'm interested in Mike Clyde. It'll just make matters worse." She put the paper back and turned toward the door. "Where is Happy Point Memorial?"

Johnny chased after her. "We're not going to a cemetery."

"I am."

"For the love of God, why?"

She turned on him. "Because I want to see if they buried the Mike Clyde that I met. Does that answer your question?"

"They're not going to let you dig him up. You wouldn't want to do that anyway." Johnny showed disgust. "He's been rotting in the ground for a month."

"Well, he looked OK when I saw him yesterday."

"Jean."

She threw up her hands. "Take me to a car rental place. I'm going alone."

He was obviously tired of arguing with her. "All right," he said. "If that's what you want."

Johnny took her to a cheap rental agency. She had her purse with a credit card of her parents' and her driver's license. She didn't let him accompany her into the building, telling him it wasn't necessary. He gave her his home phone number. He told her to call him when she was through playing with the dead boy. He seemed distracted. They said goodbye in the street.

She rented the most inexpensive car they had. It still cost her too much. She'd be paying her mom back forever. She told the man at the agency she'd probably only need it a day, two at the most. He gave her a key for a red Sentra and told her it was parked in the back. She asked for a map and directions to Happy Point Cemetery.

"You want to visit a cemetery now?" he asked, amazed. "It'll be dark in an hour."

"I don't care," she said.

He told her how to get there. The place wasn't around the block, and she knew the sun would be down before she reached the cemetery.

She drove south along the coast, away from town, the sun filling the sky with a haunting red glow as it dipped nearer to the horizon. She had the radio on loud, but she hardly heard the music. Her thoughts were in chaos. They drowned out even the beauty of the island, and her own ability to reason. Johnny was right. What was she going to do when she reached the cemetery? Dig Mike up?

Still, she didn't turn back.

Happy Point Cemetery was located on the south side of the island, on a bluff overlooking a rugged portion of the coast. Angry waves battered huge black rocks below her as Jean pulled off the main road and turned up the narrow cobbled street that led to the front of the cemetery. The soft spray from the ocean filtered in through her open window. She turned off her radio. There was a tiny bit of light left in the west, but it was failing fast. She wasn't surprised to see the wrought-iron entrance gate locked already. She glanced about, seeing no one. She turned off the car and climbed out. The red-brick cemetery walls were eight feet high, but covered with a thick growth of vines. She figured she'd be able to get in. She wished she had taken the time to buy a flashlight.

The scaling of the wall didn't prove as easy as she had thought. She tried several times and skinned both knees before abandoning the effort and circling the cemetery for an easier entrance. She found it at the back, fifty feet above the pounding waves and salty spray. Here there was a place where the wall had collapsed. The second she put her foot inside the cemetery, she became afraid. In a green hedge that ran along the back wall she found a sprinkling of yellow daisies. Kneeling, she picked a handful, hoping they would appease Mike if he wasn't resting easily.

Now, which grave is his?

The place was littered with hundreds of tombstones. Yet, even in the poor light, it didn't take her long to find Mike's spot. She merely had to look for a plot where the grass hadn't grown back yet. She found him in a cluster of trees, separate from the rest of the dead people. The branch of a weary oak hung over his tombstone, shaking leaves in the ocean wind. Jean knelt beside the recently resettled earth, setting her handful of flowers beneath the name on the granite slab: MIKE CLYDE.

The boy with the two first names.

Jean began to cry. She didn't need to dig him up. She could feel him below her. Moist mud squeezed between her clenched fingers. She could feel the pain of his last sad expressions in her chest. Why had she come here? She needed to know that his pain had been real. Now she knew it was as real as the blood that pumped in her broken heart. Tears streamed down her face and into her mouth, where she could taste their salty flavor—so much like that of the sea that had claimed him.

"Why, Mike?" she cried. "Why did you come to me?"

Then a whip of wind shook the surrounding trees. A loud crack sounded above her. Jean had only a fraction of a second to look up before the dead branch of the oak fell and struck her on the forehead, knocking her out.

CHAPTER

TEN

She was where she had been a moment ago. But nothing was the same. The sun was coming up, not going down. The air was still, the cemetery neat and tidy. She climbed slowly to her knees. What had happened? She remembered a branch falling, but when she glanced up, she could see no place where a limb had broken off. She couldn't find the flowers she had brought for Mike.

"Where am I?" she whispered.

She touched the soil beside her. That, too, had changed. The earth was looser than it had been when she arrived, as if it had just been dug up and shoveled back over a coffin.

"Mike," she whispered.

It looked so very fresh.

She stood and began to back up. "No, Mike."

Fresh as a body that had just been buried.

The brown soil on top of the plot began to stir.

"Stop it, Mike!" Jean cried.

Something poked up through the brown earth

into the air. It was a fleshy finger, attached to a muddy hand. An arm followed. It clawed for the sky as if it hoped to grab on to something.

"This can't be happening," Jean moaned. She stopped her backward retreat. She was forced to— her legs had turned to stone. She could only watch and wait and pray. A second hand emerged and grabbed hold of the tombstone. It wrapped its arm around the memorial and began to pull. A messy head burst through the ground.

"Stop!" Jean screamed.

Mike slowly climbed out of his grave. He turned to face her, his movements resembling those of a zombie. His face was powder blue. Ragged purple stitches covered the top of his skull. His brown eyes were sunken beyond the point of vision. Yet they moved, this way and that, endlessly searching the surroundings, and always coming back to rest on her. A small dirt clod was stuck in the corner of his cracked lips and he reached up to brush it away with difficulty; his fingers appeared permanently curled back. His clothes were a mess with mud, but they were the same clothes he had worn on the plane: old blue jeans, a gray shirt, olive green boots.

He didn't seem to be breathing.

"Hello," he mumbled. He coughed painfully, and more dirt came out of his mouth. "It's good to see you again."

She stared at him transfixed. "You remember me?"

"Yes. You're Jean. We met on the plane."

"And you're Mike?"

Her saying his name seemed to touch him somehow. He tried to smile, but failed—it showed only as a grimace on his face. "You remember me," he said.

"Yes. How could I forget you? What happened to you?"

The question seemed to throw him off-balance. His miserable eyes rolled to the left, in the direction of the sea, which was flat and serene. They seemed to stick there for the longest time. He had to bring them back to her with effort.

"I came here to be happy," he said.

"But you died," she said.

He could have been surprised. "Am I dead?"

Jean felt tears on her face once more. "Yes. I'm sorry."

He looked down at the disturbed grave, his own tombstone. He may have been seeing it for the first time. But understanding was in his expression, tortured though it was. He finally nodded, his crooked neck creaking like old wood in a tired house.

"I died," he agreed.

"What happened?"

"I was killed."

She took a step closer. "By who?"

"The ocean." He coughed again. "I never saw the ocean before. I told you that on the plane."

"I remember. You were looking forward to it so much. But how did you die in the ocean? Who was with you?"

"The dark fish. The cold moon." He shuddered

as if he felt a chill. More mud fell from him. "And evil. There was evil in that cave. I felt it before I went inside, but I went in anyway." He gestured her way with a stiff arm. "You did the same."

Jean nodded. "What did I see in there?"

"Destiny."

"Your destiny?" she asked.

The question hurt him. It seemed to weaken him, if a corpse could be weakened. He protested her question. "I was not supposed to die. I was killed. That's why I sat beside you on the seat. You were in my seat. You were following me, so I followed you. That's why." His sorrow was great. "That's the only why."

"No, it's not. Why were you killed?"

He lowered his head. "I don't know."

"But you must know who killed you, even if you don't know why. Can't you tell me?"

He closed his eyes at her question. She wished he would have kept them closed. When he opened them again, she noticed what a sickly green they had become, as if moss or bacteria had grown onto the eyeballs.

"I can show you," he said. Then he reached for a white balloon in his shirt pocket. It was hard for him—Jean feared halfway through the effort one of his brittle fingers would crack and fall to the ground. But finally he managed to get the balloon out. He held it up to his ruined lips. "I can show you everything I know," he said.

The balloon began to inflate. Jean didn't understand how. He was taking in no air. How could he exhale air into the balloon? It was almost as if he had a hidden regulator fed by an invisible tank. She stared at the balloon, fascinated. Once more it began to assume the shape of a heart, but this time it pulsed to the rhythm of her own heart. She couldn't take her eyes off it, and it grew and grew. Soon it was difficult to see beyond it to Mike's face. There was the heart. His heart—her heart. They were not all that different at the moment. She looked deeper into it. Or perhaps she didn't look at all, but closed her eyes and saw the truth there. It didn't matter. She was back outside the cave, back in time.

It was a night of brilliance. The night of the big moon.

The young man floated before the entrance of the cave. Gentle rays of white glittered on his face mask. He knew something about the cave. This was not his first time there. He swam inside.

He had a flashlight, and even though the moon followed him in bits and snatches through the walls and ceiling, he needed it. The beam shone before him like a beacon of sanity. But what he was doing was not entirely sane. He was diving at night to a great depth, into a cave filled with tight corners. He was far from an experienced diver. Such was the power the cave had over him. He couldn't resist. Plus he was not alone. He had an experienced partner with him. His partner was right behind him. Somewhere.

There was a surge in the cave. The moon was

strong. The tide was moving. Fish floated by the young man at unusual speed. The bubbles of his regulator raced before him, and then were sucked behind him. The kick of his fins remained steady.

The young man came to a split in the cave. He could go forward, he could go up. Or he could turn to the right. To the right was the most dangerous, the darkest. But the young man chose it because it was the way he had gone before to discover a great wonder. He glanced behind him. He could see his partner moving slowly. His partner seemed to be waiting to see which way he'd choose. The young man didn't mind.

He swam into the narrow cave. The space was tight. But he knew one more thing from his previous experience—it would soon open wide again. He was not worried. He felt great excitement. The whole island would soon know about his discovery.

The cave widened. Then the goal was at hand.

It was a skeleton. Its head bobbed in the moving water before the beam of his flashlight. But here the surge was weaker. The young man suspected the skeleton had been there for a long time, but he could have been wrong. He believed it belonged to a man who had been murdered. The hole on the side of the skeleton's head looked as if it could have been made by a bullet.

Then his partner was beside him, and the young man excitedly pointed to the skeleton. The red-suited partner was interested, but he was also worried about the time. He pointed to his watch. He wanted them to go back up. The young man didn't mind. His partner only needed to see the skeleton for a second, the young man thought, to know he had spoken the truth about it.

The two swam back up the tunnel. They entered the main cave and headed for the entrance. The surge of the tide was powerful. It was harder swimming out than it had been swimming in. The young man began to tire. He wasn't used to swimming with fins. He had learned to swim in a lake, back home. Even there he had never gone swimming at night. He wondered why his partner had insisted the dive for the skeleton be done at night.

He was about to find out.

The moment they exited the cave, the partner reached over and stopped the young man. The partner wanted to see the young man's BC hose. The young man gave it to him. After all, his partner was knowledgeable about all aspects of diving. He trusted him. Yet the young man didn't understand why his partner began to inflate the BC. They were at great depth. He knew that could be dangerous. Still, he wasn't worried. His partner had a firm hold on him.

But then his partner spun him around and took hold of the buckle on his weight belt. He began to pull the belt loose. The young man saw in a flash that his partner was trying to hurt him. If he lost his weight belt now, this far down, with his BC fully inflated, he'd shoot straight to the surface. He'd die a horrible death.

The young man tried to fight off his partner. He grabbed at his partner's wet suit and ripped it. But he wasn't strong, and his partner had the jump on him. He lost his flashlight. Then his weight belt fell off. It landed on the dark coral floor.

And then his partner let go of him.

The young man began to rise, faster and faster.

The moon shone bright above his head. It grew in brightness with each passing second. The young man began to panic. He tried turning himself upside-down. If he could swim downward, hard, he thought he might be able to save himself.

He was in the middle of turning over, when the pain started in his chest. It was crushing and immediate—a boulder could have fallen onto his ribs. He couldn't breathe. His heart shrieked in his chest. Something big and ugly was expanding inside him, tearing his guts and lungs apart. It was just compressed air, but it was more lethal than any bullet. Searing agony welled into his neck, choking off his throat. He gave up all effort of trying to get out of his predicament. There was pain, there was terror—there was nothing else. The moon swam over his head, and he raced toward it.

Seconds later he broke the surface, and the pain ceased as if cut off by a switch. He rolled onto his back and stared straight up. He could see the moon overhead, and he tried to turn to the side to find out where the shore was. He thought if he could get to the sand, he might be able to get help.

Suddenly, though, he could move no longer. All he could do was stare at the white globe as it slowly changed to deep sober red. The veins in his eyeballs had ruptured. A film of blood slipped over his vision. Then everything began to go dark. A violent slap hit his head from the inside, followed by another. The bloody moon vanished, and he understood that he was dying. Sorrow consumed his being. He thought how only a short while before he had been sitting on the plane on his way to Hawaii. He had been so happy. He had been about to enter paradise.

Then the young man knew no more.

Jean opened her eyes. "I understand now," she told Mike.

He didn't answer, his face hidden behind the white balloon. He continued to feed air into it. She knew what would happen if he didn't stop. "Mike!" she called. "Don't!"

The balloon burst. The heart. Their heart. It splattered her face with blood. The red seeped into her eyes. It cut off her sight, just as his sight had been cut off the night he died. She caught a faint glimpse of his dead silhouette. Then all went black, and she was floating on a cold sea of nothingness.

Jean came to in the dark beside Mike's grave. She felt a stab of pain in her head as she tried to sit up. She raised her hand to feel for damage. Her face was covered with blood. It was sticky but had already begun to dry. The heavy branch of the oak lay across her back. She had to struggle to get out from under it. Finally she was able to stand and take in her surrounding.

She was still in the cemetery, of course. The moon had risen; it bathed the graves in a milky glow. The wind was howling in from the sea. A chill spread throughout her body. She felt her head once more. The gash was just above her left eye, and it would need stitches, a doctor.

Then she noticed Mike's tombstone had fallen over.

It must have been the wind.

Sure.

She remembered what had happened. She remembered it all. She turned and hurried toward the hole in the wall at the back of the cemetery. She would go to the doctor later. She had things to do.

CHAPTER

ELEVEN

There was an ambulance parked outside the front of the hotel. Fear pierced Jean when she saw it. She didn't bother putting her rental car in the lot. She parked in front and tossed the keys to the valet. She hurried over to the pool area where a group of people were gathered. A moment later she saw that the police had cordoned off the area with yellow official tape.

"What happened?" she asked a potbellied man who carried a tropical smoothie in his right hand.

"Some girl jumped or fell out of her hotel room."

Jean was horrified. "Is she dead?"

"She splattered on solid concrete. I'm sure she's dead."

"Do you know who it was?"

"No. But I hear she came out of one of the rooms over there." The man pointed almost directly to Jean's room. He shook his head. "You should have heard the scream she made as she fell. It was terrible."

Jean hurried over to the yellow tape. A handsome mustached police officer stopped her before she could go under it.

"Do you know who the girl is?" Jean asked frantically.

"We haven't made an identification yet."

"Let me by," she said. "It might be one of my friends."

"I can't do that. Which room are you staying in?"

"Five-twenty-six. Which room did the girl fall from?"

"I'm not sure." He glanced up at the rooms above his head. Beyond him, close to the spa, stood a tight cluster of officers and paramedics. Jean couldn't see any body. "But I think she fell from one of those rooms up there," the officer said. "Why don't you go up to your room and check."

"Couldn't you just let me by?" Jean pleaded.

He glanced in the direction of the spa. "I don't think you want to see the body," he said grimly.

Jean traveled upstairs in a daze, praying all the way that her room would be empty. But it wasn't; it was full of cops. She walked in and fell on the couch before anyone even looked over at her. An elderly officer came and knelt beside her.

"Is this your room?" he asked.

Jean nodded. "What color was her hair?" she whispered.

"The girl had short brown hair and bangs. Do you know her?"

Jean choked on the information. Tears welled in her eyes, and she had to close them. But her tears didn't burn—they were as cold as her world, where young people she cared about could die in a moment.

"She was my best friend," she wept. "Her name was Mandy Bart."

"Do you know why she'd jump?" the officer asked.

Jean opened her eyes. She shook her head. "Mandy would never have jumped. She must have been murdered."

The cop was sympathetic. "We haven't ruled out the possibility of foul play. Let's call it an accident for now. What's your name?"

"Jean Fiscal."

"Were you here when the accident occurred?"

"No. When did it happen?"

"A half an hour ago."

"I was driving back here," Jean said.

"From where?"

"Happy Point Memorial Cemetery."

"What were you doing there?"

"Visiting a friend of mine. His name's Mike." The tears kept coming. "He's dead, too."

The cop sat beside her on the couch. He handed her a handkerchief, and she wiped at her face. "This must be hard for you," he said.

She nodded. But the nod meant nothing. She couldn't comprehend how hard it was going to be to live without Mandy. She was crying, but the news really hadn't penetrated yet. She buried her face in the handkerchief.

"Why do you say she was murdered?" the police officer asked.

"Because she wouldn't have killed herself, that's why."

"It's possible she fell. There's a faint smell of alcohol on her clothes."

"Mandy didn't drink."

"Never?"

Jean took away the handkerchief. "She would have a beer or two, but she never drank to the point where she couldn't have walked a straight line."

"Who else is staying in this room with you?"

"Michele Kala."

"Is she a friend of yours?"

"Not really. She's a girl we know at school. She came on this trip with us—I don't even know why."

"Who do you think pushed Mandy off the balcony?"

"I'm not sure," Jean said. "I suspect Michele. I suspect a guy Michele's seeing here. His name's Dave Groom. In fact, I'm pretty sure now he'd be the one who killed Mandy. He teaches scuba diving here at the hotel."

"Why do you think he'd murder her?" he asked.

Because he has a red wet suit. Because Mike's partner in the vision wore a red wet suit.

"Because I think he murdered his partner a year ago," she said. "Does the name Ringo mean anything to you? He died here on Maui a year ago under mysterious circumstances."

"What was his last name?"

"I don't know."

The officer thought a moment. "The name's familiar. Was he a guy who just disappeared?"

"Yes. Ringo was Dave's partner. Today I went diving in the spot where Ringo disappeared. A hundred feet down, in a coral cave, I found a skeleton. I came back up and told Dave, and he went down to see for himself. But when he surfaced, he said the skeleton wasn't there."

"You think he was lying?"

"I know he was lying! It was there. I saw it."

The cop took out his notepad. "Where are Dave Groom and Michele Kala now?"

"I have no idea."

"Who is this other friend of yours who just died?"

"Mike Clyde."

"Did Dave murder him, too?"

She sniffed. "Yes."

The officer suddenly froze. He closed his notepad. "How long have you been on the island, Jean?"

"I just arrived yesterday."

"Did you know Mike Clyde before you came here?"

"No."

"Then how do you know how he died?"

"I know. I read the article in the paper. I—"

"I know that article," the officer interrupted, his tone not as kind as it had been a moment ago. "In no way did it implicate Dave Groom in Mike's death."

"I realize that. But I know stuff that wasn't mentioned in that article."

"Such as?"

"I know Mike wasn't alone the night he died. I know how he died."

"How do you know this? Were you there?"

"No, I was in Los Angeles." Jean knew she was beginning to sound crazy, but she didn't know how to backtrack. She couldn't think. Mandy was dead!

"Miss Fiscal—" he began.

"You were calling me Jean a second ago," she interrupted.

"You're not making any sense," the official said. "What happened to your head?"

She had forgotten all about the cut above her eye. "A tree fell on me," she muttered, knowing he thought she was crazy anyway. She added, "I swear to you that there is a skeleton in a cave off Lanai."

"I'm sure there is." He stood. "But right now I'm concerned about the body lying by the spa. Could you come with me a second, please?"

He led her to the balcony. He spoke into a walkie-talkie. He motioned for her to peer over the edge. Jean did so. Five stories below, the group gathered around the crumpled bloody sheet parted. A paramedic pulled back the cloth to reveal the face.

What was left of the face.

Mandy must have landed on top of her head. The crown of her skull was crushed flat. The delicate bones that made up her pleasant expression were shattered. There was blood everywhere. But it was still good old Mandy. Jean could see that even from five stories up. She had to grab the railing to stop herself from falling forward.

"Is it Mandy Bart?" the policeman asked.

"Yes," she said.

"Has she family?"

"Yes."

"Would you like to notify them, or would you prefer we do it?"

"I can call her parents," Jean whispered.

"Hi, Mrs. Bart? This is Jean. Yeah, I'm here in Hawaii. Yeah, it's really beautiful. Yeah, I've been working on my tan. Mandy? Oh, that's why I called. Is she here? No, she's not. She's dead. Yeah, that's right, Mrs. Bart, your only child is gone."

"We would appreciate it if you could do that now," the official said. "We have to perform an autopsy, and we need permission. You can use the phone in the bedroom."

"Fine." Jean turned around.

"And Miss Fiscal?" the policeman said at her back.

"Yes?"

"I would appreciate it if you hung around for a while."

"I understand," Jean said.

She went into the bedroom and closed the door. She didn't call the Barts. Fishing in her pocket, she took out Johnny's number and called him instead. He answered the phone.

"Hello?"

"Johnny, this is Jean. I'm at the hotel. The police are here. Something terrible has happened. Mandy is dead."

"What?"

"She fell off the balcony. Only I don't think she fell. I think she was pushed. Johnny, it's so awful. She lying there with her head crushed. The police think I might have done it."

"Hold on a second. Why do they think you did it? Were you there when it happened?"

"No. I was on my way back from the cemetery. Johnny, I know what happened to Mike! He was murdered. He discovered the skeleton in the cave as I had and he took someone else down to see it and that person murdered him. They filled his BC full of air and ripped off his weight belt. Mike shot to the surface. His lungs exploded."

Johnny was silent a moment. "How do you know this?"

"I saw it! I saw it in my mind. A branch fell on my head while I was kneeling by the grave, and Mike came out of the ground and showed me everything. Johnny, Dave killed Mike Clyde. He killed him because Mike had discovered Ringo's skeleton."

"Jean."

"I know what I'm talking about!"

"Dave is not a killer. I've known him all my life."

"He said the skeleton was not there! But he lied! It is there!"

"Where are you?" Johnny asked.

"I'm in the bedroom in the suite. I have a ton of police outside my door. They want to keep me here. But I can't stay. I have to get the skeleton."

"This is insane," Johnny muttered.

"I have to get it now before Dave has a chance to move it."

Johnny considered. "All right, we can look into this idea of yours if we must. Can you get out of there without the police stopping you?"

Jean picked up the phone and carried it to the bedroom balcony, which was actually the far end of the living room balcony. The police were all inside. She glanced around the wall that divided her from the neighboring room. It should be a cinch to swing over to the next balcony, she thought. As long as she didn't look down.

"I can get out," she said.

"Do you still have the car you rented?"

"Yes."

"Come straight to my house," Johnny said. "Don't go chasing after Dave or any skeleton by yourself."

"Is your mother there?"

Johnny paused. "Yeah. What's my mother got to do with it?"

"Nothing. I'll come."

"You promise?"

"Yes," Jean said. She put down the phone. She wasted no time implementing her plan. She didn't want to give herself a chance to get scared. In reality, what she was attempting seemed more dangerous than it was. Standing facing out, she stepped carefully over the rail and then turned her back to the moonlit ocean. Going mainly by feel, she reached past the wall separating the rooms, and grabbed the adjoining balcony rail. In one smooth step she moved three feet to the left. Now she was standing on the outside of someone else's balcony. She quickly climbed onto it.

I hope I don't walk in on them.

Their balcony door was unlocked, and, no, they were not in. In fact, the room appeared to be unoccupied. Jean strode to the front door and let herself out. There were no cops in the hall. She dashed to the elevator and, once on the ground floor, hurried to the valet station. They hadn't even put her car away yet. The attendant recognized her. She only had to wave to him and was able to climb behind the wheel to drive away.

On the road to Lahaina she began to question her promise to Johnny.

She had linked Michele with Dave when talking to the police officer, but that had been a major leap in logic. Michele had always been kind to Mandy. It was still a possibility, but there was no reason to believe Michele was aware of what Dave had done to Mike. And if that was so, and Michele was presently with Dave, she could be in serious danger.

If she went to Johnny's house, and then the harbor, she would waste valuable time. Time in which Michele might meet with an unfortunate accident, as Mandy had. Besides, who was she fooling? She wasn't going to convince Johnny that his best friend was psycho. Johnny had said as much on the phone. Plus he would never agree to help her find the skeleton at night. And by the time they searched for it the next day, it would be gone.

I have to get it myself. I have to show it to the police. Ringo grew up on Maui. He must have dental records here. They'll be able to identify his remains and figure out how he was killed. Then they'll have to believe me.

Jean turned off the main road in the direction of the harbor. She put her rental in the same spot Johnny had parked that afternoon. She climbed out and hurried toward his boat. If she was going to Lanai, she was going to need transportation.

But Dave was working on the *Windspeed.* She spotted him before she was halfway up the dock. It looked as if he was preparing to take off. Of course, it didn't surprise her.

Going for a little late-night dive?

Jean crouched down behind another boat. She had not checked her watch since she had reached the cemetery. She was shocked to see it was after midnight. Except for Dave and herself, the harbor was deserted. The full moon glowed almost directly overhead.

She watched for several minutes, then Dave suddenly went below. This might be her only chance, she thought. She climbed to her feet and ran to the boat on tiptoes. She could be nimble when it suited her; she hardly made a sound. She climbed onto the boat at the side of the cabin. Lucky for her, Dave appeared to be in the bathroom. Quickly she searched for anything that could be used as a weapon. There were numerous air tanks stored in the rear. She hopped over to the racks and grabbed one and climbed up the ladder to the top deck of the boat. The tank felt like it weighed a ton.

It will feel a lot heavier on his head.

The downstairs head flushed. Jean stood ready with the tank over her head. A moment later Dave made his way up from the hold. One glimpse of his emerging crewcut and she swiftly brought the tank down. She caught him on the back of the neck. He let out a sharp grunt of pain and sprawled forward on the companionway. For a second she worried that she had killed him. But then she heard his deep, heavy breathing. He was snoring, of all things. He sounded as if he wouldn't be waking up in the next five minutes.

Now what?

She didn't know how to pilot a boat this size. She didn't even know how to start it. But there was another type of craft aboard that a child could have run.

The wave runners.

The twin motorcycles on water stood at the back of the boat with keys in their ignitions. She set the air tank down and walked over to them; then she crouched and checked the gas tank on the one on the right. It appeared to be full. She stood and stared out to sea in the direction of Lanai. The moon was bright on the water. There wasn't a trace of wind. She couldn't see any waves.

But there could be waves out there you can't see. You could drown.

She would be taking a risk, no doubt about it. But if she ran into swells, she should be able to turn around and come back, no harm done. Anyway, she was committed. By now the cops must be looking for her, and Dave wasn't going to sleep forever.

She made her decision. She would put on diving gear and ride the wave runner to Lanai. She would dive down to the cave. She would find the skeleton.

She would bring Ringo home, as Mike had meant to bring him home.

You're assuming it was Ringo. Mike's vision didn't say who it was.

It had to be Ringo. It was the only thing that made sense. Dave must have wanted to steal away Ringo's share of the business. He would probably be going after Johnny next.

Jean set to work.

CHAPTER
TWELVE

Thirty minutes later she found herself a mile off the coast of Maui, scuba gear on her back, the wind in her face, and the moon in her eyes. Lanai glowed six miles in front of her, a shimmering mound in a sea of reflected milk. The night was warm, her confidence high. The wave runner skimmed the surface as if powered by jets. She calculated she would reach her destination in twenty minutes.

Her mathematics proved miserably wrong. Johnny had told her how unpredictable the sea was, and that night was another example. Approximately two miles out, she ran into swells. At first they weren't that big—two or three feet. But even modest-size waves were difficult to cross in a craft that was no bigger than a motorcycle. She had to cut her speed dramatically. Even so, the wave runner bounced without mercy beneath her bottom. Many times she was tossed forward so far she feared she'd fall off. She had to cut her speed even further, cursing the ocean. At this rate it would take her most of the night to reach Lanai.

At about the halfway point the swells suddenly doubled in size. They came at her at right angles. Now she was in serious danger. Frantic, she glanced back the way she had come. Had Maui not looked every bit as far away as Lanai, she would have turned around right there. One thing for sure, she told herself, she was not going to try to come back on the runner that night. She just prayed to God she got there in one piece. The spray off the wave caps soaked over her head as the wind picked up in the eerie night. She tried to occupy herself with thoughts other than drowning, but all her mind kept coming back to was Mandy's broken body.

It wasn't fair. I never got to say goodbye to her.

Mixed in with Jean's feelings of fear and sorrow was profound guilt. From the moment of her arrival on Maui, she had cared more about her own pleasure than Mandy's. She could have turned her back on Johnny. She could have told him she had a boyfriend at home and at least given Mandy a chance. That's all Mandy had asked her for on the ride from the airport—a chance to be happy. That was all Mike had wanted.

Approximately two miles off Lanai, the waves abruptly ceased. The transition was amazing. From the angle of the swells and the placement of Lanai relative to her position, she could see that the small island must now be blocking them. She wasn't complaining. She pushed the wave runner back up to maximum speed. The remainder of the trip took her less than ten minutes. She ran the runner right up onto the sand beside the marks Johnny had left in the sand earlier that day. She had the right place, there was no doubt about it. She dismounted and checked her watch. It was two in the morning.

Her fatigue made her hesitate. She stood in the shallow water with her fins in her right hand and an underwater flashlight in her left—she had found it beside the diving gear—and once more contemplated what she was attempting. Johnny was right, it was crazy. Besides being exhausted, she was an inexperienced diver who had no experience at all night diving. She didn't even know what the water would look like in the dark. She was still on the surface, but she felt she was on the verge of stepping into the deepest of bottomless caves.

But you do know what the water looks like at night. Mike has shown it to you. He showed it to you so that you could come here at night and let the world know what happened that other night, when the moon was also full.

Jean raised her eyes to the moon. It had sunk partway off the top of the sky, but it continued to ride high. She believed its light would follow her all the way to the bottom. She would not get lost. She strode into the water.

Jean ended up doing what Dave had done earlier in the day. She did not go under right away, but rather swam out to the place where she thought the coral cliff started. She had to ration her air. She wanted plenty of time to come up slowly.

She found her spot. Then quickly she was underwater, her light in one hand, pointed downward, her nostrils pinched with her other hand. She cleared her ears continually as she descended, all the time trying to establish her bearings. She was pleasantly surprised to see that she *could* see. She dropped down thirty feet, and the glow of the moon stayed with her. She spotted the place where she had sat and contemplated going to the bottom of the cliff. She saw the ledge where she had taken her big leap into the reality of her dreams. Tonight, however, she did not pause at the top of the chasm. She went steadily down, sinking like an oxygen-breathing creature alien to a planet covered mostly with water, the expanding bubbles of her regulator floating toward the surface like silver thoughts in a silent comic strip. She prayed that in the end Mike was not playing a joke on her.

Her entire descent took her five minutes. She checked the time carefully as she stood on the bottom, along with her air gauge. Taking hold of her BC, she nudged a little air into her vest, giving herself neutral buoyancy. She had landed almost exactly where she had earlier in the day. She turned to the left, searching for the cave. But the visibility had undergone a dramatic change from thirty feet to a hundred and three feet. She estimated, even with her flashlight, that she could see no more than six feet in front of her. She would have to move forward carefully.

She found the cave shortly. Unfortunately, the dive was tiring her faster than she had expected. As in Mike's vision, the full moon had brought on the surge of the tide, and resisting its pull was difficult. She hoped its power was less inside the cave. She hurried through the dark entrance.

But the force of the tide was stronger inside the cave than out.

"No one talks about it. It's just there. It's a place. The water rushes in and it's warm. It passes through the rays of the moon. When it rushes out, it's cold."

It was cold when you came back out because you were as good as dead. That's what Mike had meant.

Jean used her free hand to grab the jagged inner wall of the cave and pull herself forward. She didn't have on her gloves. Twice she felt sharp stabs of pain in her right palm. She didn't see a single fish in the beam of her light. Maybe her light was frightening them away. Maybe the place itself did. They had seen what could happen in these waters at night.

Jean came to the tunnel. She was not going to make the same mistake as she had before. She would go straight in. According to what Mike had shown her, the place should widen out again. If it didn't, she'd back straight out. She checked her time. She'd been under ten minutes. She would stay in the tunnel no more than five minutes, and the cave as a whole only another eight. If she didn't find the skeleton in that time, it was not the end of the world. She accepted the fact that Dave could have moved it when he had gone back down.

She swam inside the narrow passageway. At first the surge hampered her. She felt as if she were in a kitchen pipe that was being attacked by a plunger. Her tank kept banging on the roof of the tunnel. The coral inside the tunnel was rougher than that in the cave. Her right hand now bled freely. With her luck a shark would probably show up.

It was no dream. I knew. I was right.

The tunnel suddenly widened, just as the force of the surge lessened. She was able to swim forward quickly. So far there was no skeleton, and she was deeper inside than she had been that afternoon when she had gotten stuck. But she was not dismayed. It was doubtful that Dave would have taken the skeleton out of the tunnel in the short time available to him. Then it could have been spotted by any local diver. He had probably buried it farther inside the tunnel, figuring he could dispose of it for good when the tiresome girls from L.A. were gone.

Jean had to reevaluate her theory a minute later. The tunnel dead-ended in a narrow crevasse that a sea turtle couldn't have passed through, and still there was no skeleton. She turned around, scanning the area. Where could Dave have stuffed Ringo?

It was then she caught a glint of white out of the corner of her eye. She moved up and to the right. There was another narrow crevasse, even narrower than the one the cave dead-ended into. Sticking out of it was a skeleton hand.

Hallucination, my ass.

She now had confirmation that Dave had purposely moved the skeleton.

Jean checked her time. She had been in the tunnel three minutes. She had to get out in the next two. She pulled on the bony hand and yanked it right off.

Sorry, Ringo.

She floated up as high as possible, pressing the top of her head on the ceiling. She peered down the crevasse. He was all there, all right. But she didn't need all of him. The skull alone had the bullet hole, his teeth. She set her flashlight on the coral and reached forward with both hands, grabbing him by the lower jaw and the back of the skull. The bony material felt slimy beneath her fingers. She gave a hard yank. His head came off in her hands.

I am really sorry. Maybe we can put you back together later.

Jean tucked the skull under her arm and picked up her flashlight. Then she turned and started back down the tunnel. She concentrated on her leg kick, trying to keep her knees from bending. She needed speed, but more important, she had to conserve her energy and oxygen. The surge gripped her once more. She had to squeeze the skull tightly. She couldn't be free of the impression the tide was trying to knock it out of her arm.

Finally she reached the cave proper. This time she was careful to turn to the left. She felt a powerful elation. Mandy was dead, but she was going to get the bastard who had killed her.

She had just exited the cave and was about to start her ascent when a hand grabbed her from behind.

Mike!

But it wasn't Mike. It was a flesh and blood hand. It was no doubt the same hand that had killed Mike. Her flashlight was knocked away. The skull fell from her arm. Her assailant carried no flashlight of his own. All went dark, and in the dark Jean felt herself spun around and around. Her regulator was ripped from her mouth. She grappled for it frantically, and as she did so, she felt her BC hose pulled to the side. Air flowed into her vest. The hand fell to her weight belt.

He's doing to me what he did to Mike!

Before Jean could do anything to stop him, she knew she had to get the regulator back into her mouth. She found it floating directly above her head. She had to force herself to purge the water out of it before she began to breathe off it. But by then she was too late. She had taken in only one decent breath when she felt her weight belt slip off her hips. The hands that had attacked her let her go.

She began to rise toward the surface. Quickly.

God help me!

God was not going to help her. God had invented buoyancy and pressure, fragile lungs and hearts. She would have to help herself. She remembered her vision of Mike's death vividly, what he had failed to do. The overriding factor that was contributing to her buoyancy was the air in her BC. She had to dump the air, while simultaneously swimming down. She reached for her BC hose. Her terror reigned supreme. Yet her reflexes remained sharp, her senses alert. The watery moon shone above her head. The brighter and clearer it became, she realized, the more certain her death became.

Jean found the button that released the air from her vest and pressed down on it firmly. A second stream of bubbles erupted around her. She tucked in her head and did a half somersault, still holding on to the button. Her fins were now pointed at the moon. She kicked furiously. A dull pain formed in the center of her chest. But the moon stayed where it was, coming no closer. The bubbles pouring out of her BC hose ceased.

I have to go back down and come up slowly.

She did not want to go straight back down, however. Dave was there. Even without her flashlight, he might spot her. He could send her racing to the surface again. Or, since she was proving uncooperative, he could take out her regulator and let her breathe salt water. The pain in her chest remained. She turned to the left, still kicking hard. Even without the air in her BC, she was extremely buoyant without her weight belt. Her best bet was probably to get to the bottom and put a few rocks in her vest pouches. She hoped she knew when she got to the *right* bottom. The moonlight shimmered all around her, but it was not strong enough to allow her to read her pressure gauge. If she accidentally missed the second ledge, she could swim down two hundred feet and not know it.

Breathe deep and slow. Conserve your air. Don't freak out.

Jean headed back down. The pain in her chest began to ease. She realized that her ears were also aching. She pinched her nose and blew lightly. The pain in her left ear only got worse. She suspected she had damaged her eardrum. Well, there was no helping it. She was lucky to be alive—boy, was she lucky.

She reached the bottom a minute later and immediately grabbed on to the first thing she felt, which fortunately was a ledge of sorts. The water was the blackest blue imaginable. The moon was visible above the surface, but it looked a million light-years away. She groped around with her free hand. She came up with a handful of sand and poured it into her pouches. She felt her buoyancy lessen and dumped in more. Soon she could sit comfortable on the bottom without having to hold on to the ledge for support. It was while she was resting and catching her breath that she saw the circle of light a hundred feet off to her right begin to move toward the surface.

Dave.

He didn't see her, or if he did, he gave no sign of it. She wondered if he'd see her bubbles once he reached the surface. Certainly he'd notice that she was not lying dead as Mike had. But if she could come ashore a ways down from where she had entered the water, she might be able to sneak away from him. It was her best hope.

Jean turned and began to swim to her left, moving slowly upward as she did so. When she was about halfway to the surface, she stopped and waited for three minutes. Then she swam up to fifteen feet and waited another three minutes. Here she was able to read her depth and air pressure gauges. Her tank was almost empty; she rationed what air she had left as best as she could.

When she finally came up, she checked out the surrounding area immediately.

The *Windspeed* was anchored a hundred yards away from her, in the opposite direction from the underwater cave, about thirty yards offshore. She could see no one aboard. Keeping her head down, using her snorkel, she swam toward the shore. She felt slightly dizzy, but she believed she hadn't damaged her heart or lungs. She just hoped she didn't get the bends later.

The beach was narrow. Where the sand ended, a bunch of bushes began. Removing her fins, she scampered over to the bushes and immediately sat down. It felt good to be on solid ground again. She unhooked her gear and rested for a few minutes. The night was comfortably warm, even though she was sitting in wet shorts and a blouse. She had not had her bathing suit with her when she had brained Dave at the harbor.

The question of the night kept returning for a different set of circumstances. Now what? She got up on her knees and peered at the boat again. There was still no sign of Dave. Why had he left the boat? The beach for that matter? When he came up and didn't see her, he should have stayed and searched for her. Of course, it was possible he was hiding in the bushes as she was, waiting for her to show herself. She sat listening for another few minutes, but no significant sound came to her ears.

Curiosity began to get the best of her. She picked up her mask, snorkel, and fins. If she swam straight back out, and circled around, she should be able to peer into the boat and see what was happening without his knowing it. Taking a last quick look around the beach, she stood up to dash across the sand and back into the water.

It was then someone tapped her on the shoulder.

"Oh!" she gasped.

"Shh, Jean. It's me. Johnny."

He sat beside her in the bushes. Her relief in that moment was so great, she collapsed into his arms. "Oh, Johnny," she whispered. "Where have you been?"

"Where have I been?" he whispered back. "Where have you been?" He gestured to her diving gear piled beside her. "You haven't been back down in that cave, have you?"

"Yes! I dived back down and found the skeleton. I was carrying it to the surface. Then I was attacked by Dave. He pulled out my regulator. He inflated my BC and yanked off my weight belt. He tried to kill me!"

"Hold on," Johnny said. "Are you sure it was Dave?"

"Yes!"

"Did you see his face?"

"No. But who else could it have been?"

"If you didn't see his face, it could have been anybody."

"I know it was Dave. The skeleton is down there. He lied about it being there. Trust me." She paused. "How did you get here?"

"The same way you did, I think. When you didn't show up at my house, I figured you had gone to the boat. I drove there as fast as I could. I noticed one of the wave runners was missing, and some scuba equipment." He shook his head. "You must have been insane to try to cross the ocean on a runner."

"You've done it."

"I did it again tonight. I took the runner instead of the boat because it's faster, and I thought I could catch you before you went too far. But you must have had too much of a head start on me."

"Where is your wave runner?" she asked.

"Just around the bend. Wait! Who's that coming?"

A white figure was emerging from the bushes, heading in the direction of the boat. She reached the shoreline and waded into the water.

"Michele," Jean gasped.

"She must have come with Dave on the boat," Johnny said.

"When you went to the boat, did you see Dave?"

"No."

"But I knocked him out," Jean said.

"You knocked him out? You are something. Well, he must have woken up and gone for Michele." Johnny frowned in the direction of the boat. "Are you serious he tried to kill you?"

"I wouldn't make it up!"

"No, I mean, if Dave wanted to kill you underwater, you should be dead."

She put her hand on his bare leg. He had on a black wet suit vest. "I'm tougher than I look," she said.

Johnny was indecisive. "He must be aboard the boat. If what you say is true, I have to stop them. Do you think Michele is in on this with him?"

"Yes," Jean said.

"All right, let's plan. We'll swim straight out

from where we are and circle around and come at the *Windspeed* from the sea. That way we can take them by surprise."

"Do you think you can handle Dave?" Jean asked.

"If he doesn't know I'm coming, yeah."

Johnny didn't have a mask or snorkel with him. He told her not to worry, she'd have to keep up with him. Together they scurried across the sand and into the water just as Michele climbed onto the boat. They swam out a hundred yards beyond the boat before they began to swing back toward it. Jean was more tired than any human being had a right to be, but somehow she managed to keep up with Johnny.

The *Windspeed* rocked gently in the calm waters. Fifty feet off its bow, Johnny motioned for her to stay where she was. He went forward alone, swimming silently up to the hull. He used one of the boarding ladders to pull himself up so he could peek over the rail. What he saw must have satisfied him. He suddenly jumped aboard, disappearing temporarily from Jean's view. She heard a shout, a cry. Then there was silence. Johnny reappeared on the deck of the boat and waved to her to come aboard. She almost sank with relief. It was finally over.

She saw two crumpled bodies as she climbed up the ladder. Michele was near the cabin, lying unconscious against the door. Dave was sprawled in the rear—close to Jean—facedown in a pool of blood. Dave looked the worse of the two. Jean was not even sure he was breathing.

How could he have bled so much so quickly?

"Is everything OK?" she asked uneasily as she removed her fins. She pushed her mask and snorkel up on her forehead. Johnny stood in the midsection of the boat. He gestured to the victims of his surprise attack.

"I did what you told me to do," he said.

Jean knelt beside Dave, feeling his neck for a pulse. She found one, but it was weak. His breathing was faint, rapid, and shallow. Jean glanced at Michele. The girl was showing no signs of stirring.

"We're going to have to get Dave to a doctor," Jean said.

"We'll get him one."

Jean stood. Something wasn't right. She couldn't pinpoint what it was. "Did you have to hit them so hard?" she asked.

"I don't know. Did I?"

"What are we going to do now?" she asked.

"What would you like to do?"

"Head back to shore immediately," she said.

"What about the wave runners?" he asked.

"Let's leave them."

"All right," he said. He stared at her. "What's the matter?"

"Nothing. I'm just worried about these guys."

"Why?" he asked. He took a step toward her. "They tried to kill you."

"I know, but I hate to see people hurt." She grimaced. "Especially after what happened to Mandy."

"I understand."

She glanced down at Dave again. She could see

he was still bleeding from a head wound. She needed to find something to bandage it with. "Do you have a first-aid kit aboard?" she asked.

"It's below."

"Could you get it?" she asked.

"All right." Johnny reached over his head. "Let me get this suit off first. It makes me sweat."

He pulled his black wet suit off. It was red on the inside.

Jean stared.

"Is that suit yours?" she asked.

He slowly peeled it from his arms. "Sure."

"I thought I saw Dave wearing one like it today."

"Sometimes he wears my suits. I hate it when he does."

"You need someone to sew this up for you."

"Or I need to lose some weight."

"You're not overweight."

"I know."

At the time Dave's last remark had made no sense to her. Now she could see that he had been implying that he didn't have on his own wet suit.

"Does Dave have a red wet suit?" she asked softly.

"No. Why?"

"I was just wondering."

Johnny stepped down into the rear section and stood near her. "What's the matter?"

She kept her gaze fixed on the sea. On the reflecting moonlight. She had seen so many secrets in its rays, and yet she had seen so little. She had seen Mike's partner, the suit he wore. But never his face. She slowly turned to Johnny. She had to fight to keep her voice even.

"I want to take one of the wave runners back," she said.

"Why?"

"Because it's faster. I'll get there before you." She stammered. "I can call the hospital and have an ambulance waiting."

"I can call the hospital right now on our CB," Johnny said. "Besides, that would be too dangerous." He reached out his hand and touched her chin. His touch was cold. "You're trembling."

"I know."

"Why?"

She forced a smile. "I've had a hard night."

He moved his hand on her chin to the back of her neck. Slowly he turned her so that she was facing him. He put his other hand on her shoulder. He pulled her closer.

"I never got to kiss you last night," he said.

She lowered her head and swallowed. "You can kiss me later."

"But I want to kiss you now." He leaned over and spoke in her ear. She still had her mask on. "Don't you want to kiss me?"

"Yes. But—"

"But what?"

She shook her head. "But this is not a good time."

His head moved back. "Why not?"

Tears started to burn into her eyes. She fought them back. She raised her eyes to his, then back down to his sly grin. Once upon a time she had thought it an innocent smile of amusement. Now she could see it wasn't innocent at all, but extremely calculated.

She could hardly breathe. But wasn't that what this was all about? A monster who took a person's own breath and turned it into a knife through the heart. A knife wound that left no evidence.

"Let's get going," she said. "I want to go home."

His voice was suddenly flat. "Home is a long way off. You know that. You know too much. Sit down, Jean." He pressed down on her shoulders. He used all his strength, which was greater than most people would have guessed, even his partner. She sat down beside the rail of the boat and the body of Dave. "You're not going home," he said.

CHAPTER
THIRTEEN

Johnny sat across from her. He left Dave lying in the middle. There may have been a symbolism in the gesture, but if there was, it was lost on Jean. They sat in silence for a whole minute, which was a long time in Hawaii. In a Hawaiian minute you could go from the bottom of the ocean all the way to the surface. You could break your heart. Jean could feel her own heart breaking.

"I guess you want to know why," he said finally.

"No," she whispered.

He leaned forward. "I want to tell you."

"Why?"

"So you'll understand."

"I don't want to understand."

He showed anger. "You think you know everything already, don't you? Since the time you got here, you've been telling everyone about stuff you didn't even see."

"I can see," she said.

Her remark quieted him somewhat. He began to fidget. "Do you want to hear the story or not?"

"No."

"Damn you! I'll tell you anyway. I needed the money. It's as simple as that."

"Mike and Mandy had no money," she said.

"It wasn't their money I needed. It was the *Moonflower*'s." He looked off in the direction of the underwater cave, then back at her. His expression was an unusual combination of confusion and bitterness. He seemed to be lost, a child who had done something bad and didn't know how to avoid being punished. Yet he also seemed capable of great violence. There was indifference in his eyes.

"The buried treasure," she said sarcastically. But she decided she wanted him to talk. She needed time to figure a way out of her predicament, and talking could give her that. Plus, strange as it might sound, she was curious as to what had led him to such extreme behavior. "Did Ringo find it first?" she asked. "Is that why you had to kill him?"

His anger remained. "We found the safe at the same time. It was in a hundred and eighty feet of water. As you know by now, that's deep. No one can stay down that deep for long without special mixtures of gas. And we couldn't get those without arousing suspicion. You see, everybody was searching for stuff in these waters. The safe was heavy, and it had half a wall of plywood attached to the back. We decided our best bet was to float it up to the surface using balloons. But we had to do it at night. No one could know. You know why."

"Because the money didn't belong to you," Jean said.

"It may as well have belonged to me as belonged to the fish."

"Did Dave know?"

"No."

"Why not?"

Johnny shrugged. "It just would have been one more person we had to split with."

"What went wrong?"

"Everything. That Ringo—what a bastard. Even as we were getting our gear together, he started joking about how since I was only eighteen, I shouldn't get a full share. He laughed and said maybe, if I was nice to him, he would cut me in for ten percent. He was so full of himself. He thought he was set for life. But he was wrong. The first night we went down, we brought an extra tank with us to inflate the balloons. These were not party balloons; they were more like rubber buoys. But we didn't have enough of them to get the safe buoyant. The thing was so heavy we figured it must be loaded with gold. We had to come back the next night with more balloons." Johnny paused. "I brought a gun."

"You were just being cautious, right?"

"He was going to rip me off! What would you have done?"

"I wouldn't have killed him. Why did you need money so desperately?"

Johnny lowered his head. "I didn't. My mother needed it."

"Right. You did it all for the sake of your poor mommy."

He glared at her. "That's right. My mother doesn't drink—she gambles. She's sick. She can't stop. Football games, horse races—it doesn't matter to her. She has half a dozen bookies. She owes them all, and these guys are not patient. In fact, they can be pretty nasty. They make her work the money off. Do you get my meaning?"

Jean remembered his mother—that jerk. The whole family was sick; it must be genetic.

She chuckled. "That's pitiful," she said.

"Shut up," he swore.

"All right." It was foolish to taunt him but hard not to. She glanced around. Unfortunately, there was no harpoon gun sitting within arm's reach. In fact, the only thing she had near her besides Dave's unconscious form were her fins. Her mask and snorkel were still pushed up on her forehead.

What good will they do me? I couldn't outswim Johnny.

Was that true? Johnny had told her yesterday that even a poor swimmer with fins could outrace a great swimmer without fins. And she was not a poor swimmer. Still, she'd have to get a head start and figure out where she was supposed to swim to. At the moment there weren't a lot of danger-free zones in the area.

"What happened when you came back for the safe?" she asked.

"We went down and attached more balloons. There was a full moon that night. The tide was surging. The safe began to lift off the bottom. I could see Ringo all jazzed up through his face mask. He was already thinking of the hot car he was

going to buy. It pissed me off. I took out my gun."
Johnny shrugged again. "He didn't feel a thing."

"You shot him in cold blood?"

"I shot him because he was going to take what was mine. What's wrong with that?"

"Nothing," Jean said. "You did the right thing."

"I told you to shut up."

"What happened to the safe?"

"It got away from me."

"How?"

Johnny was disgusted. "I had it all the way up to fifteen feet. I was hovering at that depth like I was supposed to. But nearer the surface the surge of the tide was strong. The safe slipped away from me. It was no big deal, I thought. I could just grab it again. But then a couple of the balloons came loose. Ringo hadn't tied them tightly enough. Before I could get a hold on the safe, it began to sink. I swam after it, but it went down like a rock. Then it was just gone."

"Gone? Why didn't you just go back down and get it?"

"I couldn't go back down immediately. I had to stay on the surface for at least two hours to let the nitrogen flush out of my system. I couldn't risk getting the bends. I still had to get rid of Ringo's body. Then, when I did go back down, I couldn't find the safe. I searched the area, but I couldn't search that much. The only light I had was from my flashlight. I had to start back up in five minutes. Besides, I already had a feeling the safe was gone for good."

"Why?"

"There was another cliff right beside where we originally found the safe. The bottom of it's over four hundred feet. I think when the safe sank back down, it went over that cliff."

"That's really sad," Jean said sympathetically. "All that work for nothing. So you stuffed Ringo in the cave?"

"In the tunnel in the cave. In a crack in the wall at the end of the tunnel. I never thought anyone would find the body in a thousand years." Johnny sighed, and there was bitterness in the sound. "But Mike Clyde found him."

"How?" she asked.

Johnny was puzzled. "I'm not sure. It appears to have been a combination of things. The motion of the tide must have knocked Ringo's body loose after a while. By then there wasn't much of him left. The fish will eat anything. Ringo's skeleton was floating around in the tunnel when Mike happened to float in."

"But why did he swim into such a tight spot? I would never have swum in there unless—" Jean didn't finish.

"Unless what?" Johnny asked sharply.

"Never mind."

"No, I do mind. How did you know to go in that one cave?"

"I told you, I dreamed about it."

Johnny put his hands to his head and squeezed his hair. "Damn."

"Mike told you he also had a dream about the cave?"

Johnny shook his head. "This is supernatural.

Yeah, he took a short scuba class at the hotel like you girls did, then he wanted to go for a dive out here. He didn't have much money, but he offered to help us get the boat ready for the cruise and clean it up when we got back to port. Dave said, What the hell. We took him. But then he approached me after we had dived in the cove. He wanted to dive at this spot. I asked him why. He said he had to. I told him no way, he wasn't experienced enough. But he came back out here on someone else's boat a couple of days later. He faked them out, convinced them he was certified. They let him do what he wanted." Johnny kept shaking his head. "He dived down to the cave and found Ringo. I was lucky he didn't tell anyone else on the other boat about it."

"Why didn't he tell them?" Jean asked.

"He didn't know any of them. But he knew me. He trusted me. I had helped teach him how to dive. It was after he found the skeleton that he confided in me about his dreams of the cave. I didn't know what to think. I was spooked. But he was all excited. He wanted to show me the skeleton. I said all right, but we had to go there at night when no one else was around, and he had to keep quiet about it until we were sure the skeleton was real. I told him he might have been hallucinating. Mike was a trusting guy. He did what I said."

"Then you took him down there, inflated his BC, and ripped off his weight belt."

Johnny was astounded. "How do you know that?"

"I saw it in a dream," she said simply. "Like Mike."

Johnny wasn't buying it. "There's got to be a logical explanation for this. That goddamn cave can't be haunted."

"It may not have been haunted before you stuffed Ringo in it, but it's haunted now."

"I told you to shut up," he growled.

"You tell me to shut up when I say something you don't like. How come Dave didn't see the skeleton when he dived down to the cave?"

"Because I had moved it. I saw your bubbles coming out of the cave this afternoon. I swam in after you. I was close to the tunnel when you came bolting out. I could see you were scared. You were going the wrong way to get out of the cave. I wondered if you had seen the skeleton, if it had gotten loose again. After Mike's discovery, I had stashed it in so that there was no way it could get pulled free by the tide. But as soon as I went in the tunnel, there it was again. I just couldn't figure it out. I stuffed it back at the end of the tunnel and swam out of the cave and waited for you."

It sounded as if Ringo had wanted out of the cave.

"Why did you stop me from rushing to the surface?" she asked. "I could have died right there and then, and your problems would have been over."

"You probably wouldn't have rushed to the surface so quick that you would have died. At the most you would have gotten the bends. Besides, I didn't want to kill you. I wasn't sure you had seen the skeleton, and even if you had I thought I could convince you that it had just been a hallucination caused by nitrogen narcosis. But you refused to drop the matter." Johnny was thoughtful for a moment. "You kept talking about your dreams, like Mike had."

"Why did you kill Mandy?" she asked.

"Besides Dave, she was the only witness to the discovery of the skeleton. And Dave didn't believe it was there."

"Is that the only reason? Mandy didn't believe I saw it."

"Yeah, she did. After I left you at the car rental agency, I went back to your hotel. She was there alone. I talked to her for a couple of hours. She was convinced something was going on. She told me about your dreams. She said she had always thought you were psychic."

"She never told me that." Jean's tone hardened. "What did you do, throw her off the balcony?"

"I got her a little drunk first. But, yeah, that's about the size of it. Then I left the hotel and went home."

He spoke of the deed in such a normal tone that she knew he was psychotic. He would try to kill her, there was no question about that. She began to get an idea about a good direction to swim. She inched her hand closer to her fins.

"How did you end up here?" she asked.

"I came after you when you didn't show up at my house. I found Dave unconscious in the boat. I saw that one of the wave runners was gone. I figured out what you were up to. I put on my dive gear and got on the other wave runner. I even passed you on the ocean. You didn't see me. You didn't see Dave behind us."

"How did he know to come after us?"

"There's a powerful pair of binoculars aboard this boat. He must have spotted us on the water. Michele could have just happened by. Dave must have thought we were crazy trying to make the cross between the islands when there were waves. If there hadn't been waves, we would have been way ahead of him. But as it was, he got here not long after you."

"You got here before me?" Jean asked, surprised.

"Of course. I watched you dive under. Then I saw Dave approaching in the boat a couple of miles offshore. I decided to take care of you first. I thought I'd have no problem." He paused. "How come you didn't die?"

"I told you, I'm tougher than I look."

Johnny wasn't going to argue with her. "When I resurfaced, I couldn't find your body. I didn't know what was going on. Dave came in and anchored the boat. Michele went ashore to look for you. Dave was preparing to search for both of us. I swam over and said hi. Then I belted him when he turned his back. I went looking for you again and found you in the bushes." Johnny stopped. "That's the story, I guess."

"And now what?" she asked, resting her left hand close to her fins.

His voice became flat again. "Now I just have to clean up a few details, and I'll be done."

Jean laughed at him, although she felt far from

happy about what he had just said. "You're an idiot, do you know that? You've left a trail a mile wide behind you. You think you can just kill the three of us out here and get away with it? The police are probably on their way here right now. I told them all about the skeleton in the cave."

"I doubt they believed your story. Even if they did, they won't come out here till tomorrow morning. And by then there'll be no skeleton in the cave. There'll be no Michele, no Dave, no you, and no *Windspeed*. I'll sink this boat in deep water on the other side of the island and take one of the wave runners back. No one saw me enter the harbor, no one will see me leave. There will be no evidence to accuse me of anything. My mother will swear that I spent the entire night at home."

"Your mother's a tramp! Who'll believe her?"

Johnny jumped up. "Don't you bad-mouth my mother! You understand that!"

Jean grabbed the fins and jumped up, too. She had Dave between them—Johnny couldn't simply reach out and grab her. She wanted to get something off her chest.

"I understand that you're both dirt!" she yelled. "I feel dirty just being near you." She spit in his face. "Goodbye, Johnny. I've got to wash myself off."

And with that, Jean pulled down her mask and dived overboard.

She swam downward and then curved back, under the boat. Above her she heard Johnny dive in the water after her. But he was already fooled. The moon was still bright in the sky, but it was dark under the *Windspeed*. He swam away from the boat, searching for her. She slipped on her fins and swam in the opposite direction.

It was her plan to swim horizontal to the beach, away from the boat, and when she was sufficiently out of sight, to make a dash for the shore and the bushes. Admittedly it wasn't much of a plan. The main problem with it was she didn't have on her scuba equipment. She had to stay near the surface and stay visible with her fins making a lot of noise as they flapped in the water. Still, it was better than staying on board and waiting to be clobbered to death by an air tank.

Jean swam as hard as she could away from the bow of the boat with her face in the water, using her snorkel. She did this for several minutes, using her arms as well as her fins. Then she was exhausted. She had to pause and peek over her shoulder. At first she was surprised to see that Johnny was not on her tail. Could she have fooled him so easily?

It was wishful thinking. Johnny knew exactly where she was. But rather than chase after her in the water, or use the boat, he had dashed ashore for the wave runner she had ridden over from Maui. Jean listened in horror as he turned on the runner. The roar of its engine echoed over the water. He was going to try to mow her down!

He was on her in seconds. The sight of the front end of the wave runner heading straight for her was unnerving. She dived underwater. The noise of the engine made her ears ring as it slashed only a couple of feet above her head. She resurfaced and wasn't surprised to see Johnny turning sharply around. He was coming in for another run. He was laughing! She dived back under. When she came up, he was turning again. She gasped for air. Her chest burned with exhaustion. She had to do something!

Johnny made four more runs at her before she caught sight of something that might save her. She was about two hundred feet off shore. Below her feet the water was over a hundred feet deep. But not far away was an isolated coral bank. About ten feet across, it protruded off the underwater cliff wall and came within a foot or two of the surface. It was true Johnny knew these waters well, but she reasoned that he couldn't possibly know every part of the reef. Besides, he was riding the wave runner like a Harley-Davidson, shouting and cursing at her. He was out of control.

Jean dived under once more as he made another pass at her, but this time she didn't come straight up. Instead, she swam toward the bank of coral. The wave runner sank a ways into the water, particularly with a person on it. If she got in front of the coral, and he came at her again, and then she dived under, he should crash into the bank.

Jean swam as far as she could underwater, but had to come up far short of the coral. A glance over her shoulder showed Johnny turning for still another run. He screamed at her as he straightened up.

"You're dead meat!"

Perhaps because she had gone underwater and stayed there for a bit, Johnny had ridden farther away from her than the previous times. Consequently, this time he had a longer approach to build up speed. As he bore down on her, she strained to get nearer to the coral. The closer she was the better, because he usually cut speed right after passing her. She doubted he could see the coral. She had only seen it because she had been forced to keep diving underwater and had a mask on.

"Bitch!" Johnny yelled.

Jean reached the coral when Johnny was less than thirty feet away, a small distance for a wave runner with the accelerator pushed to the limit to cover. She whirled in midstroke, preparing to dive under. Then she saw Johnny do the most remarkable of things. It was truly bad karma for him to do what he did at precisely the moment he did.

While riding over to the second diving spot that afternoon, Johnny had tried to impress her by "hotdogging" on the wave runner, which meant standing up on it while going at full speed. On a flat lake, that wouldn't have been difficult, but on the bouncy ocean it required either guts or stupidity. She had not been impressed with the stunt and had immediately pulled him back down. Well, he was doing it again, and she still wasn't impressed. Of course, this time she wasn't going to pull him back into his seat.

Jean dived underwater.

The wave runner roared over her head.

Then there was an awful crash.

Jean popped up just in time to see Johnny flying headfirst into the shallow bank of coral. The wave runner had done a complete flip. He didn't even have a chance to throw his arms in front of him. He struck the water and the coral in probably the same hundreth of a second. She heard a distinct cracking sound. It was not the sound of shattering coral, but of snapping neck bones. It was what she had been hoping for. Still, she had to close her eyes to it.

When she opened them again, the wave runner was lying on its side with its engine off. Johnny was floating facedown in the water. Despite all he had done to her and others, she wanted to go to him and help him. There was a possibility he was still alive. But she simply didn't have the strength. The tide was taking him out, and she couldn't go out after him. Weary to the bone, she turned toward the boat and swam lazily on her back. Above her the moon was still shining, as it had a month before for Mike, and a year before that for Ringo.

Dave was sitting up in the rear section as she climbed aboard the *Windspeed,* his hand to his head. He moaned as he surveyed the puddle of blood spread around him.

"Is that mine?" he asked.

Jean removed her fins and pushed up her mask. She hurried to his side and knelt and tentatively touched his wound. Behind her she could hear Michele snoring comfortably.

So they both snore when they've been hit over the head with air tanks. They must be compatible.

"You poor dear," she said. "Just sit here. I'll go below and get the first-aid kit."

"Do you know where it is?"

"Actually, no. Where is it?"

"In a drawer beneath the lower bunk bed." He took her arm before she could leave. "Do you know I've been hit over the head twice tonight?"

205

"I know." She felt guilty. "I hit you the first time."

He winced and let go of her arm. Leaning back, he closed his eyes and moaned again. "Please don't hit me again right now. I don't think I could take it."

"I won't. I didn't mean to hit you the first time."

He suddenly opened his eyes and stared up at the moon. "Johnny hit me the second time," he whispered. "Where is he?"

Jean knelt close to Dave's right ear. "He's dead."

Dave snapped his head around to stare at her. He started to respond, but then he relaxed. When he spoke next, it was as if he were far away.

"That was Ringo down there that you found today," he said.

"Yes. Johnny killed him. He killed Mike Clyde, too, because Mike found Ringo's remains."

Dave sighed. "I believe you. I knew, I guess, a part of me knew. But I didn't want to believe he would do such a thing."

"Johnny killed Mandy, too."

There were silent tears in Dave's eyes, big tough Dave. "I'm sorry, Jean. I truly am. I should have stopped him before. I knew he was bad. I just kept hoping he'd grow into something decent. I thought you could help him." He coughed in pain. "We'd been friends since we were kids."

Jean patted Dave's shoulder. "It wasn't your fault." She gazed out over the ocean. Far away she could see Johnny's lifeless body slipping beneath the surf. She wondered if they should even go after it. Perhaps his death should be lost in the water, in the sea where he had thrown away his life. Johnny had been crazy, that was all there was to it. She thought of the call she still had to make to Mandy's parents, what she would say. "It was nobody's fault."

EPILOGUE

Jean leaned with her head against the oak that stood guard above the grave. The day was calm, the sky bright. Green grass had begun to sprout through the brown soil that covered the fresh earth. The warmth of the sun on her bare arms and legs was like a massage. She rested with her eyes only half open. She didn't see Mike come up, but when she turned, she found him sitting beside her.

"Hi, Mike," she said and smiled.

"Hi, Jean," he replied.

He had gotten a tan. He had on bright blue swimming shorts and a baggy Hawaiian T-shirt. His hair looked lighter, as if the sun had bleached it. He looked relaxed, happy.

"Am I awake?" she asked.

"No," he said, his southern accent soft and clear. "But you're not asleep. You came here to say goodbye to me. I have come to say goodbye to you, and to thank you."

"Why are you thanking me?" she asked.

His warm brown eyes were far away, as they had been on the plane, but now they were free of sorrow. "When we met," he said, "I was lost. I didn't understand where I was. I knew something bad had happened that I was not happy about. I wanted to tell you about this bad thing, but at the same time I didn't want to talk about it."

"Because when you talked about it you felt as if it was happening to you again?" she asked.

"Yes." He bowed his head and shrugged. "It wasn't an easy way to die."

"I know. Why did you choose me to talk to?"

"I woke up on the plane. I saw you sitting in my seat." He was embarrassed. "I thought you were pretty. Besides wanting to tell you about the cave, I wanted to get to know you." He smiled. "That's one thing that makes me glad. I feel I have gotten to know you." He glanced over at her. "But you look unhappy."

She nodded, wiping at the tears that had suddenly come into her eyes. "I remember how I felt on the plane, how pleased I was when you were there, and how horrible it was when you left. It was so sudden— it felt all wrong. Now you're here and I'm here, but I know you'll be gone again." She gestured with her hand. "It just hurts, you know, that none of this can last."

She expected Mike to nod sympathetically, but his smile only broadened. "It lasts, Jean," he said gently. "It lasts forever. I understand that now. You cleared up my unfinished business for me, and I'm no longer confused." He reached out and took her

*hand. His touch was like the warm sun, only strong-
er. "We are together in this moment. It is only the
narrowest of veils that will separate us when this
moment passes. It doesn't have to separate us at all
if we remember that good things never die. Our
friendship was brief but sweet. It will endure, you'll
see."*

*Jean nodded. She was still crying, though, but it
was because she wanted to cry. "I miss Mandy," she
said.*

*Mike laughed softly. "You may miss her, but I
haven't missed her."*

Jean brightened. "You've met her?"

*He nodded and took back his hand. "Yes, and I
think our friendship will be very long." He laughed
at something only he knew and stood up. "Don't
look for me in any more dreams. I won't come. I
don't want to bother you. No, don't get up. Stay
where you are. Live where you are. We'll see each
other again when we see each other. That will be at
the best time. Now, close your eyes. Someone is
calling your name."*

"But—?"

"Goodbye, Jean. You've done well."

*She didn't exactly close her eyes, but she blinked,
and in that moment he vanished. So did the sun and
the grass. It was all gone.*

But it was still all there. Jean opened her eyes.

"Jean!"

Dave and Michele were walking up the narrow
grass-lined path that led to Mike's grave. They had
dropped her off at the cemetery a little while

earlier. They understood that she wanted to be alone beside the grave to say goodbye to Mike, or at least they pretended to understand. But maybe she had been there longer than she knew. They were waving for her to get going. Their plane left for Los Angeles soon. They were taking Mandy home, four days before their vacation was supposed to end.

Jean sat up and stretched. She had fallen asleep beneath the oak that had landed on her a couple of days earlier. But, of course, she hadn't been asleep at all.

"I'm coming," she called. She went to stand, but it was then she spotted the gold necklace lying in the soil near where Mike's tombstone had been set up again. It was a tiny angel, a gift Jean had given to Mandy two Christmases ago. Jean held it in her hand in the warm sunlight. As far as she knew, Mandy had not brought the necklace with her to Hawaii. Jean looked up at the sky, where far in the distance she could see a jet plane leaving the island, disappearing into the clear blue, perhaps going to another paradise.

"Thanks, Mike," she said.

Look for Christopher Pike's
Whisper of Death

About the Author

CHRISTOPHER PIKE was born in Brooklyn, New York, but grew up in Los Angeles, where he lives to this day. Prior to becoming a writer, he worked in a factory, painted houses, and programmed computers. His hobbies include astronomy, meditating, running, playing with his nieces and nephews, and making sure his books are prominently displayed in local bookstores. He is the author of *Last Act, Spellbound, Gimme a Kiss, Remember Me, Scavenger Hunt, Final Friends* 1, 2, and 3, *Fall into Darkness, See You Later, Witch, Die Softly,* and *Bury Me Deep,* all available from Pocket Books. *Slumber Party, Weekend, Chain Letter, The Tachyon Web,* and *Sati*—an adult novel about a very unusual lady—are also by Mr. Pike.